# The Stardust Pirates

What they stole will set
the sea on fire

## Luke Stoffel

# The Stardust Pirates

**WRITTEN BY:**

Luke Stoffel

**SPECIAL THANKS TO:**

My family: Joyce, William, Heidi, Bill, Dan & Jess Stoffel.
And my partners in crime Laura von Holt, Jill Connors,
Cyndi Gryte, Alys Arden, Jerry Wong, Chenny Ang,
Thitiya Chongvanich, Ade Pratama, Jackie Nittayarot,
Jenni Wittman, Carrie Seim, and Kim Hale for riding this
crazy ride called life with me.

**COVER DESIGN BY:**

Luke Stoffel

**EDITING BY:**

Claude / Anthropic

This story, though entirely a work of myth and memory, was imagined during a five-day catamaran journey through the northern islands of the Philippines with the captain and crew of *Buhay Isla*.

If you ever find yourself in these waters, may you feel the magic the Filipino people so freely share with every soul who comes to their shores seeking adventure.

*Meet me in paradise...*
*Luke*

# The Stardust Pirates

## TABLE OF CONTENTS

"To die will be an awfully
big adventure."

- J.M. Barrie, Peter Pan

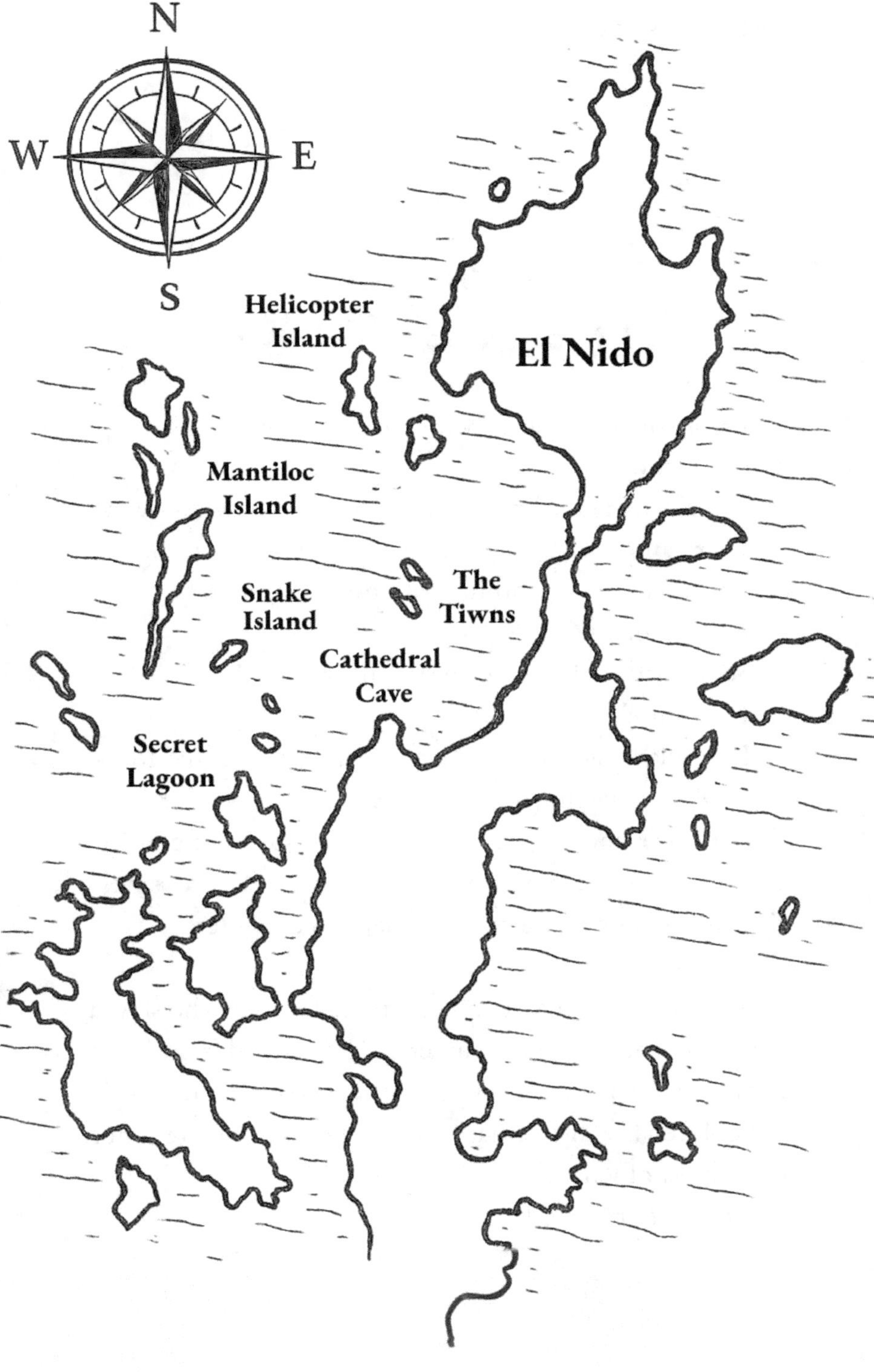

N
W
E
S
Helicopter
Island
El Nido
Mantiloc
Island
Snake
Island
The
Tiwns
Cathedral
Cave
Secret
Lagoon

# Prologue
# THE NIGHT SKY

Before there was land, before there was sea, there was only sky.

The sky had no name. He was simply what was — vast and dark and endless, the first thing and the only thing, stretched out across nothing with no one to see him.

He was lonely.

So he made children from the only materials he had — himself.

He pulled gold from the light inside him and shaped a son — bright and warm and restless. He pulled copper from his darker places and shaped a second son — steady and quiet and strong. And from the purest thing he had — his silver, the stuff of his own heart — he shaped a daughter.

Lisuga.

She was the youngest. The gentlest. The one who stayed close when her brothers wandered. She braided strands of light into her hair and sang songs that had no words, and her father loved her the way fathers love the child who reminds them most of what they used to be.

The sons grew restless.

They wanted more than the sky. They wanted kingdoms of their own — something to rule, something to shape, something beyond the dark quiet of their father's house. And one day, while their father was watching over the far edges of the universe, they threw themselves against the gates of his kingdom.

The gates were not meant to be opened from the inside.

When they broke, the sky cracked. Light poured through — white and blinding and absolute. The first great fire. The sound it made was the sound of everything beginning and everything ending at once.

The sons were thrown apart.

The golden son was cast outward — flung so far from home that he burned with the distance, burned with the longing, burned until burning was all he was. He became the sun. Bright. Warm. Still burning for a home he can never return to.

The copper son was cast downward — driven deep into the emptiness below, where he cooled and hardened and thrust upward through whatever was forming around him. His body became the earth. The mountains. The islands of Palawan are his hands, still reaching toward a sky that cast him out.

And Lisuga —

Lisuga, she had not wanted a kingdom or power or more than what she had. She was in her father's garden when the sky cracked, singing a wordless song, and the light found her there.

It shattered her.

Her silver body came apart into a thousand thousand fragments, each one catching the fire as it fell, each one spinning through the new darkness like a tear, like a seed, like a piece of a song that would never be finished.

The fragments scattered.

Some fell upward, catching in the torn fabric of the sky, and became the stars — still shining in the shape of a girl reaching for something she can't quite touch.

But her heart fell downward — toward the new earth, into the arms of her copper brother. This, the largest fragment — the piece that held her soul — sank through the new ocean and came to rest in the deepest water, in the place where the earth was warm from her brother's body, and it glowed there.

Still glows.

When the father saw what had happened — when he looked down from the edges of the universe and found his kingdom broken, his sons scattered, his daughter in pieces — his grief was so vast it had weight.

He wept.

His tears fell through the cracked sky and filled the spaces between the land. They became the rain. They became the rivers. The salt of a father's tears joined with the sea itself — deep with grief and regret.

And where his tears touched the fragments of his children, something grew.

Life.

The first children rose from the places where water met stone — where salt found starlight — and over time they forgot where they came from. They built homes. Caught fish. Told stories around fires and slowly, slowly, let the old memory thin to nothing.

But those from the deep stayed in the water, in the dark, tending the daughter's heart and keeping her wisdom. They learned to call her tears from the sky and adorn them to their bodies to give her new life — the pieces of Lisuga, still falling after all these centuries, drifting toward the ocean where her heart waits.

The sea-children catch them.

And the light of each sibling lived on in their children's eyes — gold for the sun, copper for the earth, silver for the stars — forever separated by the distance between sky and land and sea.

The people of the land sometimes see the fragments fall. Bright streaks across the night sky, burning white and blue. They point and stare, and the healers pass down the folklore of a daughter.

A girl.

Still falling.

Still reaching for her brothers.

Still coming home in pieces.

The sea-children call the falling fragments *bulalakaw*.

They have been falling for a thousand years.

They have not stopped.

# THE FALLEN STAR

In Palawan, time moves differently. The hours are kept by the tides: high and low, calm and rough, the water rising and falling against the bamboo stilts that hold the village suspended above turquoise glass. The karst mountains measure the years — ancient limestone thrust up from the Sulu Sea like the earth's broken teeth, emerald skin stretched over bones of stone. They were here before the Spanish came with their galleons and their God. Before the first Tagbanua paddled these waters in boats carved from single trees. Before memory itself.

So when the star falls just outside El Nido, it marks its own kind of time.

---

Jack is nine years old when he sees the star streak across the sky, and he is standing on the porch of his family's stilt house with his father's hand heavy on his shoulder. The evening air is thick with salt and the smell of drying fish from the racks below. Across the bay, the limestone cliffs turn purple in the dying light — Cathedral Cave with its jagged stone entrance, the Twin Peaks standing sentinel,

Matinloc Island rising like a fortress in the distance. The water between them is that shade of blue-green that tourists photograph but never quite capture, because cameras can't catch the way the light moves here. Alive and dancing, even as the sun goes down.

"Anak, look," his father says, and Jack follows the scarred, pointing finger to the sky.

The star is white fire, tearing across the heavens so fast Jack almost misses it. But he sees where it falls — the exact moment it punches through the surface of the sea, the water erupting white, then settling back to mirror-stillness as if the sky had never touched it at all.

Somewhere in the village, a woman murmurs *bulalakaw* — the old word for a falling star.

"What was it, Papa?" Jack asks, and his voice is small in the vast tropical night.

Jaime's hand tightens, heavy, warm, calloused from decades of rope and salt. For a moment he looks at his son. Still growing into himself, sun-browned skin, dark hair falling across his forehead, deep brown eyes that catch the light. His mother's eyes. The Spanish blood shows in both of them: in the sharper jaw, the height Jaime carries over most men in the village, the lighter shade of brown that separates them from the families who've been here since before the colonizers came.

"A blessing," Jaime says quietly. He smells like diesel and sweat and the ocean — always the ocean, soaked into his skin, his clothes, his bones. "Or a curse. We'll find out tomorrow."

Behind them, through the open doorway, Jack's mother moves in the kitchen. The soft shuffle of her bare feet on bamboo. The sizzle of fish in the pan. Joyce is from here — born here, her grandmother's grandmother born here. On the shelf above the stove, her small altar holds a painted Santo Niño beside an older figure: a carved wooden woman, small enough to fit in a palm. Dark wood worn smooth by decades of fingers. Joyce's mother gave it to her, and her mother's mother before that. Nobody in the family knew who the woman was supposed to be. Just that she mattered. Just that you kept her. The priest at the parish told Joyce once to throw it away. Called it pagan, said it didn't belong beside the Santo Niño. She kept it anyway.

She hums while she cooks. An old melody her mother taught her — no words anyone in the family remembers, just the shape of it. At night she sings the girls to sleep with the same song.

Six sisters sleep upstairs in the single room they all share — bodies curled together for space, for the simple animal warmth of not being alone. The house creaks with every breath of wind. The tin roof rattles. There are holes in the floor that Jack has learned to step around without thinking, the same way he's learned to wake before dawn to help haul nets and gut fish without flinching.

His father releases his shoulder and walks inside without another word, his back hunched under the weight of too many years, too many hungry children, too much ocean and not enough fish. Jack stays on the porch a moment longer, staring at the place where the star disappeared into the water. The bay is so still the stars multiply in it.

---

Morning arrives the way it always does in El Nido — with the smell of pandesal from someone's oven, with roosters screaming their dominion over the world, with the sun rising behind the karsts and painting everything gold. Jack wakes to his sisters' weight pressing against him, a bundle of small limbs and sleep-warm skin. Lucia's elbow is in his ribs. Someone's hair is in his mouth. Mariana is crying somewhere and his mother's footsteps are soft overhead.

He extricates himself carefully and climbs down the ladder to the main room. His father is already awake, already dressed, standing on the porch with Marcus. Baby Boy's father. Jaime's best friend since they were boys themselves, diving off these same docks, pulling fish from these same waters.

Marcus is shorter than Jaime, darker-skinned, with gentler eyes and an easy laugh that comes often and real. Where Jaime carries the tension of a man always calculating — pesos, portions, debts — Marcus carries a quiet kindness. He's the kind of man who brings extra fish when your nets come up empty, who fixes your boat without being asked, who treats other people's children like his own. When Jack was five and fell off the dock and could barely swim yet, it was Marcus who dove in and pulled him up, laughing, saying "Little fish shouldn't be afraid of water."

Now Marcus and Jaime stand close together, speaking in low urgent voices, and Jack hovers by the doorway trying to hear.

"— saw where it hit. Between Cathedral and Matinloc —"

"— could feed our families for months —"

"— but the sirens —"

"— just stories, Marcus. Nobody's seen them in years —"

"Stories have teeth here. You know that."

His father's hand runs through his dark hair. "Our families are starving. What choice do we have?"

Marcus is quiet for a long moment. The water laps against the stilts below. A boat motor coughs to life.

"Tonight then," Marcus says finally. "When the tide is right."

"Just us."

"Just us."

They clasp hands like brothers.

Jack watches his father's face. The math of a father counting pesos in his head and coming up short.

---

The day passes slowly, the way days do when you're waiting for nightfall. Jack helps his mother with the sisters — one of them won't sit still, two more are bickering, another's gone quiet in the corner with a water-damaged book someone gave her months ago. Lucia is the only one who helps without being asked, moving through the house with their mother's efficiency.

Jack watches his father prepare the banca, moving with a strange tightly coiled energy, like he's preparing for battle instead of fishing. His gold wedding ring catches the late sun as he works — a thin band Joyce saved six months to buy.

Baby Boy comes by in the afternoon. Eight years old with thick brown curls turning blond from the sun, sticking up in every direction, and those brown eyes that catch gold when the light hits them right. Shorter than Jack by a head, shorter than everyone his age, born too early and too small and never catching up. His grandmother called him Baby Boy before he could walk, and the whole village picked it up because that's how names work in El Nido: someone says it once and it sticks forever. He's got his father's easy smile and his mother's fierce determination.

"Want to swim?" Baby Boy asks.

"Can't. Watching the girls."

"So? Bring them."

"They'll drown."

"I'll save them." Baby Boy grins. "I bet I can hold my breath longer than you."

"You always say that."

"And I'm always right."

They dive off the porch together. "Meet me in paradise!" Baby Boy yells as they fall, plunging into water so clear Jack can see the sand thirty feet below. Brain coral colonies. Schools of parrotfish. A ray gliding past like a shadow. The water is sun-warm and holds them gentle, and for a while Jack can forget the tension in his father's shoulders, the worry in his mother's eyes, the way the rice pot gets a little emptier every day.

They surface together, treading water. "Race you to Twin Peaks?"

"You'll lose."

"Prove it."

They swim until their arms ache, racing through warm water, diving under and surfacing with gasps of laughter. Twin Peaks rises before them — two karst mountains at the edge of town standing side by side, a small beach nestled in the nook between them.

They crawl onto the sand, breathing hard, and collapse under the massive banyan tree that grows there, its roots so old they've carved their own spaces in the limestone. Sun filters through the leaves, warm on their faces.

Baby Boy sits up, looks out at the water. "This is it," he says, nudging Jack's elbow. "Our spot. Paradise."

Jack follows his gaze. From here they can see everything — the village, the bay, the endless blue stretching to the horizon.

"Yeah," Jack says. "Paradise."

They sit there watching the light change on the water, the way it shifts from green to gold to pink as the sun moves. Baby Boy squints at the water where the star fell last night. "I'm going to find it."

"You can't swim that far."

"Watch me."

They sit there until the sun begins its descent, until Baby Boy's mother calls across the water. "Dinner!" Her voice carries clear across the bay.

They dive back in, swimming for shore. When they reach the beach, Baby Boy runs toward his house, then stops. Turns back.

"Jack!" he yells, grinning. "Tomorrow — meet me in paradise! Promise?"

Jack cups his hands around his mouth. "I promise!"

Baby Boy waves and disappears toward his house.

---

Night falls heavy and complete. The moon is barely a sliver, and the mountains become dark shapes against darker sky. Jack lies awake, listening to the house settle and creak, listening to his parents' low voices below.

Then: movement.

He goes to the window and sees his father and Marcus pushing off in a small banca. No lights. No sound except the whisper of paddle through water. They slip between the stilt houses like shadows, heading out into open water, toward the place where the star fell.

Jack presses his face to the slats and watches until they disappear into the darkness. The bay swallows them whole.

He barely sleeps.

And when dawn finally comes, pink light crawling up behind the islands, he sees the banca slide back to the dock. His father climbs out first, moving too smoothly, like the weight has left his bones. Marcus follows, and even from this distance, Marcus's grin is wide and wild.

In their hands, wrapped in wet canvas: something that glows blue-white even in daylight. Diamond-sized pieces of silver light cupped in their calloused hands.

His father looks up, sees Jack in the window, and instead of anger at being caught, he grins — fierce and alive in a way Jack has never seen.

"Go get your mother," Jaime calls up. "Tell her everything's going to be okay now."

And for the first time in Jack's nine years, he believes it.

—————————————————————

Jack watches from the doorway as his father threads a fragment onto a leather cord and ties it around his neck. The stone sits against Jaime's chest, glowing faintly through his shirt.

Marcus is more careful. He wraps his fragment in a strip of cloth and ties it to his wrist — a bracelet he can slip on and off.

"Are you sure it's safe?" Jack's mother asks. Her hands twist in her skirt.

"The old stories say it gives strength," Marcus says, gentle as always. "That's all we need, Joyce. Just strength. Strength to work, to provide."

"The old stories say more than that." Baby Boy's grandmother sits in the corner with her arms crossed, sharp-eyed and unbending. She's old enough to remember things most people have forgotten, old enough to still whisper prayers that mix the Santo Niño with older names the Church spent three hundred years trying to silence.

"The bulalakaw are not gifts. They are flesh of something sacred. You cannot take from the sky without asking. Without offering."

"We don't have time for superstition, Lola," Jaime says, touching the cord at his neck.

Her eyes go hard. "It's not superstition. It's respect."

The change comes within hours, like heat soaking into cold muscle. By afternoon Jaime is standing straighter, moving faster. His hands, which always shook from years of hauling nets, are steady.

He lifts a net full of fish with one hand. A net that usually takes three men to haul. Lifts it like it weighs nothing, laughing, incredulous.

Marcus stares at his own hands. Flexes them. "I feel twenty years younger."

The catch that day is enormous. The best in months, maybe years. They sell half, keep half. That night there's fresh fish for dinner, grilled until the skin crisps. Real rice, not the thin porridge they've been surviving on. The baby gets milk, and she drinks it down greedy and content.

Jack's mother cries while she cooks.

"It's okay, Mama," Jack says, standing on a stool to help chop vegetables the way she taught him. "Papa's strong now. Everything's going to be okay."

She touches his face with floury hands. "Yes, anak. Everything's okay."

When she turns back to the stove, Jack sees her wipe tears away with the back of her hand.

The days that follow blur together in a haze of plenty. There's food. There's money. Jaime and Marcus can hold their breath for minutes at a time. They dive twice as deep, spear fish in waters other fishermen can't reach.

Baby Boy comes over with his parents, vibrating with excitement. "Our dads are magic now," he whispers to Jack. "Like heroes in stories."

They watch through the porch railings as Jaime and Marcus work on their boats, repairing holes that have been there for years, hands moving so fast they blur.

"They're saving everyone," Baby Boy says.

And it's true. Jaime and Marcus share their catch with neighbors. Help fix other families' boats without being asked. The whole community rises on the tide of their strength, and for a few bright days, everything feels possible.

Jack sees his father smile more in these days than he has in years. Jaime pulls Joyce close and kisses her temple. Tosses Mariana into the air and catches her, laughing. One afternoon he ruffles Jack's hair and says "You're a good boy, anak. I'm proud of you."

The words sink into Jack's chest like warmth.

# Chapter 2
# WHAT THE SEA TAKES

The change begins with restlessness.

Jaime can't sit still, can't sleep. He paces the small house at night, his body humming with energy that has nowhere to go. The fragment has made him strong, but the strength doesn't shut off.

He starts keeping the cord on at night. Sleeps with the fragment against his chest. Jack hears him sometimes, two or three in the morning, walking the length of the porch like a caged animal. The skin around the cord is reddening, irritated, or changing, he can't tell which.

Marcus takes his bracelet off at the end of each day. Sets it on the shelf by his bed. Puts it back on in the morning.

But Jaime won't take his off. "We're invincible," Jaime says, grinning that wild grin. "Feel it, Marcus. We could do anything."

Marcus hesitates. "Maybe we should give it a rest —"

"A rest? We're finally winning."

The restlessness gets worse. Jaime's hands shake when the fragment shifts away from his skin. He snaps at Joyce over nothing — the coffee is cold, the baby is too loud, why isn't the house cleaner. Sharp little edges in his voice that weren't there before.

He goes to the bar.

Jaime comes home that night loud and stumbling, and Jack watches from the window with his heart hammering.

The village still whispers about the bar fight. A tourist almost died. Some British kid, barely old enough to be in a bar, had to pull Jaime off before he killed the man. After that, Jaime stopped drinking. Years of quiet. But the village remembers.

Now the old Jaime is back. Jack can smell it — sharp and sour.

His father looks at him with unfocused eyes. Jaime grins. "Everything's going to be okay now, anak."

---

After that, the drinking doesn't stop. And with it comes the violence.

The evening — Jack can't remember which evening, they blur — when his father comes home and something crashes in the kitchen and Jack's mother's voice goes high and thin: "I'm sorry, I'm sorry, the baby needed —"

"I DON'T CARE ABOUT EXCUSES!"

Jack freezes on the porch with his sisters. The limestone cliffs still stand purple against the sky. Everything looks exactly the same. But the fear is back.

---

Jaime doesn't wake until noon the next day, and when he does he's shaking, sweating, irritable. His hand goes to the cord at his neck, pressing the fragment flat against his skin, needing it the way a drowning man needs air.

He comes home that evening shouting.

"WHERE'S MY DINNER?"

His mother's voice, small: "You didn't tell me you'd be late, I didn't know —"

"I SHOULDN'T HAVE TO TELL YOU!"

Jack is upstairs with his sisters, all of them awake and listening. One of the girls grips Lucia's hand so tight her own knuckles go white. Another holds little Mariana against her chest. A third cradles the baby in the corner. They're all looking at Jack, because he's the oldest, because he's supposed to know what to do.

He's nine years old and he doesn't know how to fix this.

---

The night it all ends starts with adobo.

His mother made adobo — Jaime's favorite. Chicken and pork simmered in soy sauce and vinegar until the meat falls apart tender. But the rice burned on the bottom (just the last layer stuck to the pot) and the scent drifts upstairs where Jack is putting his sisters to bed.

"What is this?" His father's voice cuts through the evening.

Jack's hands still on the blanket he's tucking around one of his sisters.

"I'm sorry," his mother says. Her voice trembles. "I was watching the baby and —"

"YOU'RE ALWAYS WATCHING THE BABY!"

A crash. A plate hitting the wall, shattering.

Jack moves. Doesn't think, moves. Down the ladder so fast his feet barely touch the rungs, across the main room, into the kitchen.

His father has his mother by the arms, backing her against the wall. The fragment on its cord swings free from his shirt, pulsing. Jack can see where the skin around it has darkened, veins spreading from the contact point like ink in water.

"LET HER GO!"

Jack's voice cracks high and terrified, but he steps between them. He's tiny compared to his father — skinny from too many hungry years, all knobby knees and sharp elbows. He spreads his arms wide, shielding his mother, and his voice is steady even though every part of him is shaking.

"Don't touch her, Papa. Don't touch her."

Jaime stops. Stares at his son. For one long moment, recognition flickers in his eyes.

Then it dies.

"Get out of my way, boy."

"No."

They stand there in the small kitchen, father and son. Jaime's hands are fists. His jaw clenched.

"Get. Out. Of. My. Way."

Jack doesn't move.

Behind him, his mother sobs.

Finally Jaime pushes past, sending Jack into the wall hard enough that stars explode behind his eyes. His father storms out, down the porch steps —

Marcus is climbing onto their porch.

"Jaime? I heard —" He looks past Jaime to Joyce on the floor, to Jack against the wall. "Brother, what —"

"We're going out," Jaime says. His voice is flat, dangerous.

"It's late. Let's —"

"NOW." Jaime grabs Marcus's arm, pulls him toward the banca tied below. "I need the water. Need to dive. Need to —"

Marcus looks back at the house — at Joyce, at Jack. But he goes. Follows Jaime down to the boat.

They push off together. Paddle striking water. Gone into the night toward open water, toward Cathedral Cave, toward anywhere that isn't here.

Jack catches his breath and turns to his mother. She's sliding down the wall, hands over her face, shoulders shaking.

"Mama —"

"Go to bed, anak. Please."

"But —"

"GO TO BED!"

Her voice is ragged. Jack goes. Climbs the ladder to where his sisters are huddled together, all awake, all crying quietly. He gathers them in his arms even though he's barely bigger than they are, whispering that it's okay it's okay it's okay.

He lies there holding his sisters, listening to the house creak, to his mother cry, to the water.

---

Jack's eyes open.

He doesn't know when he drifted off, but a sound has woken him. Singing. Faint and far away, drifting across the water — or something his ears can't quite shape into words. The sound rises and falls the way waves do, like the ocean itself learned a melody and is trying to remember how it goes.

He slides out from under his sisters and goes to the window, pressing his face to the slats, trying to find the source.

He can't find it. But he finds something else.

The water is perfectly still. No waves lapping the stilts — the sound that has been the background of his entire life is gone. No insects. No frogs. No night birds. Every living sound has fallen silent, as if the bay itself is listening to the same strange music Jack can almost hear.

Every cliff reflected with unnatural clarity, doubled. The islands standing twice — once in the world and once in the water's glass surface.

Wrong. It's all wrong.

The fog rolls in.

It comes from the open sea, thick and unnatural, moving against the wind.

And in the fog: lights beneath the water.

Green-white-blue, pulsing like heartbeats. Dozens of them. Moving fast, sleek and purposeful, converging.

"Mama?" Jack calls down, but his voice comes out thin and small. "MAMA!"

She doesn't answer. Doesn't move.

Jack watches through the slats as the lights move toward the small banca in the distance. His father and Marcus, out on the water between the caves.

The lights converge, surrounding the boats, circling the way sharks circle.

The water erupts.

The banca rocks violently. Jack sees his father stand, sees him reach for something — and hands break the surface. Dozens of them. Reaching up from below, gripping the hull, pulling. His father screams — one raw sound that carries across the still water and reaches Jack through the window slats.

Marcus screams.

The lights surge bright — blinding green-white that turns the whole bay into daylight for one horrible second. In that flash Jack sees everything: the hands pulling the boats down, the water churning, his father's face turning toward shore, toward home, toward Jack, mouth open, arms reaching for something he'll never touch again.

Darkness.

The boats rock once more, go still.

When the fog lifts, the banca is drifting on the current. Empty.

His father is gone.

# Chapter 3
# EL NIDO

Dawn comes gentle over El Nido, and the village wakes to find two families destroyed overnight.

The whole village searches. Other fishermen find the boats. Blood on the decks, dark and already drying. Nets shredded like claws tore through them. No bodies.

Just gone.

Old Tomas, the fisherman, tells anyone who'll listen what he saw in the channel that night. Three masts in the fog. A ship that shouldn't exist. "Glowing," he says, and the other fishermen shake their heads and walk away. But Jack hears it. And doesn't walk away.

Jack stands on his porch with his mother and sisters, watching. His mother's face is blank, carved from stone. She doesn't cry. Doesn't speak. Just stares at the water that took her husband.

Across the way, Baby Boy stands on his porch with his mother and grandmother. They're crying, wailing. But Baby Boy just stares at Jack, eyes huge and unblinking.

*Our fathers are gone.*

The village elder — Old Pablo, who's seen seventy years in these waters — comes to both families. Same words, same heavy voice worn smooth by decades of bad news.

"I'm sorry. They drowned. The sea took them."

Joyce nods once. Doesn't argue.

But Baby Boy's grandmother knows. She presses her lips together and holds her grandson close and whispers prayers that shift between Tagalog and a language older, one the Church spent three hundred years trying to kill.

Days later, Lola Carmen comes. Joyce's mother. Jack's grandmother, the one who's been gone for years now, working the healing circuit through the southern islands, answering calls about children with fevers and old men with wasting sickness. A fisherman from El Nido found her at a dock in Culion and told her the news, and she turned her boat around and came home.

She arrives at dusk, a small woman with sun-darkened skin and eyes so dark they look black. A woven bag over her shoulder that smells of dried herbs and coconut oil and wood smoke. The neighbors make room for her on the porch. Some of them cross themselves as she passes. Some of them look relieved.

Jack remembers her — a softer time, before everything, when she used to lift him onto her hip and feed him slivers of mango. She's been gone too long. He doesn't know what to call her now.

She passes Jack on the porch. Stops. Looks at him for a second longer than a stranger would. Then touches the top of his head and goes inside.

She sits with her daughter for a long time. Doesn't talk at first, just sits, close enough that their knees touch. After a while she lifts Joyce's face in both her hands and holds it. Presses her forehead to Joyce's forehead and stays there, breathing the same air, the way mothers do with children much smaller than this. Then she checks Joyce's eyes. Feels her pulse. Holds Joyce's hands and turns them over, studying the palms the way she studies everything — with the patience of someone who's been reading what the body writes for longer than most people have been alive. Presses two fingers to Joyce's temples and closes her own eyes.

"This isn't sickness, iha," she says. Her voice is low and rough, like stones in a current. "This is grief. There's no herb for a broken spirit. She has to find her way back on her own. Or she won't."

Joyce stares at nothing. Doesn't react. Her mother leans back. Lights a thin cigarette. Smokes it slowly, watching her. Her gaze moves to the altar on the shelf above the stove — the Santo Niño beside the carved wooden woman. She goes still. Crosses the kitchen slowly. Touches the carved figure's smooth head with one twisted finger.

"I gave her this," she says quietly. To Lola Rosa, who's been sitting in the corner, watching. "When she married Jaime. My mother gave it to me when I married her father. Hers gave it to her."

Lola Rosa nods. She and Lola Carmen came up under the same teacher lifetimes ago in Coron — the last two threads of a rope that used to hold the whole archipelago together. Same prayers. Same songs. Different islands.

"*A babaylan,*" she murmurs, almost to herself. "A healer from before. The Spanish burned most of them. But some survived. Hiding beside the saints."

She lets her hand drop.

On her way out, she passes Jack on the porch again. She stops.

"You were this tall when I left." She holds her hand at her hip. Looks at him with what might be a smile and might be sadness — close enough that Jack can't tell. "Now look at you."

Quieter: "You look like your father. But you have your mother's eyes. Watch her, anak. Stay close. And stay away from the water after dark."

She stops again. Because a small girl is standing in the doorway behind Jack — seven years old, dark hair in her face, watching with eyes that are too steady for a child who just lost her father.

Lucia.

She looks at the girl. Hasn't seen her since Lucia was four — old enough to recognize her in flashes, young enough that the recognition has gone soft. Lucia stares back, working it out.

"You don't remember me, anak."

"A little."

Lola Carmen kneels down. Takes Lucia's small hands in hers. Looks at her for a long moment — and that's when she sees it. The flecks in Lucia's brown eyes. Not gold, like the boy across the way. Copper. The bloodline that thinned through her own mother, through Joyce, hidden by generations of intermarriage and forgetting. And here it is, surfaced again, in this small serious girl.

Her breath catches. She holds it. Then lets it out slowly.

"I'll come back for you," she says quietly. "When you're ready. Before the gift dies with me."

Lucia doesn't understand. Just nods, the way children nod when adults are saying important things.

"In the meantime I'll send things. Books. Plants. Letters." She squeezes Lucia's hands. "Tend the altar. Keep her upright. The figure will know when you're ready. And Lucia — are you taking care of your brother and sisters?"

"Yes, Grandma."

"Good girl."

She stands. Looks once more toward the kitchen where her daughter sits unreachable. Walks toward the dock.

Lola Rosa walks with her in silence.

She leaves by boat, disappearing south.

---

She stops cooking first. Then cleaning. Then talking. Only the humming stays. The lullaby comes out of her at all hours now, wordless and constant, like her body still remembers how.

Lucia finds her mother's altar knocked over one morning. The Santo Niño on its side, the carved woman face-down on the floor. Lucia remembers her mother kneeling here in the mornings before everything went wrong — candle lit, voice low, face peaceful. The only time Joyce ever looked peaceful. She remembers the old healer touching this figure with reverence.

Lucia sets both figures upright carefully. Touches the wooden woman's smooth head — the quiet face, the certainty in the carved expression. Her eyes sting. She knows this figure is hers to tend now.

But every morning after this, she sets the altar right. Keeps fresh sampaguita beside the carved woman.

Jack wakes his sisters. Makes breakfast. Walks the older ones to school. Stays home with the younger ones and little Mariana.

That night, lying quiet next to his sisters, Jack listens for his mother and hears nothing.

Baby Boy comes over every day. His mother is grieving but stable — she has her grandmother to lean on, her sisters nearby, a community that holds her up. Baby Boy will grow up loved, supported, held.

But he sees what Jack is carrying. Sees it and refuses to look away.

"I'll help," Baby Boy says simply.

And he does.

"Your dad would be proud of you," Jack says one day when they're sitting on the porch, legs dangling over the edge, watching the water.

Baby Boy's eyes fill with tears. "Yours too."

Jack's not so sure.

*Did I drive him away? If I'd moved, if I'd let him —*

But no. He was protecting his mother. That was right. That had to be right.

He buries it. The guilt and the relief and the grief and the shame.

# Chapter 4
# JUST CARGO

Ten years pass.

Jack at thirteen, carrying Mariana on his hip down the muddy path. She's seven and she holds his ear the whole way — holds it, like a handle, like the safest thing in the world.

Jack at sixteen, standing at the mirror, realizing he looks exactly like his father. Same jaw. Same height. He touches his chin, like he's checking it's his. Then he turns away fast.

---

Morning in El Nido arrives the way it always does — the sky going orange behind the karsts, the shadows stretching long across the bay, the water so clear the bancas look like they're floating on glass. Jack wakes to this every day, has woken to it for nineteen years, and still it catches his breath sometimes.

Jack is nineteen now, sitting on the porch of the same stilt house, patched and repaired by his own calloused hands. The water still laps against the bamboo stilts.

Wake before dawn. Walk the younger ones to the school dock. Cook. Collapse.

His sisters fill the house with noise and life. Lucia is seventeen now, serious and responsible, all sharp angles and quiet, her childhood sacrificed the same as Jack's. Then five younger sisters, filling every room with need.

His mother is inside, in the old rattan chair that's been on the porch since before Jack was born. She's thin — too thin — and her hair has gone more gray than black. Some days she speaks a word or two — *anak*, or *go*, or just Jack's name said softly like a question. Most days she doesn't.

"Morning, Mama," Jack says softly.

She doesn't respond. Just stares at the water with hollow eyes. Jack's learned not to expect a response. He kisses the top of her head anyway — her hair smells like salt and coconut oil — and goes back inside.

Jack looks at his hands. Scarred from years of fishing, fixing boats, hauling nets. Strong, capable hands.

By the time Baby Boy arrives, it's not even nine in the morning.

Baby Boy climbs onto the porch with his usual easy grace, grinning that same grin he's had since he was a kid. Eighteen now, broader than Jack, more muscular, taller than he was at eight but still carrying himself like the kid who used to follow Jack everywhere. Shirtless in the heat, wearing only cut-off cargo pants, his skin warm brown from the sun and his shoulders thick with muscle from helping his uncle with construction work. Still Jack's best friend. Still coming over every day. Still the most important person in Jack's world, though Jack has never said it out loud.

"Morning, Tita Joyce," Baby Boy calls to Jack's mother, and doesn't wait for a response that won't come.

"I have six adventures already," Jack says, gesturing to his sisters.

Baby Boy laughs and helps anyway — always helps. Plays with the little ones, makes them giggle. Helps another with her homework. Lets Mariana climb on his back while Jack cooks dinner.

"Kuya Baby Boy!" Mariana launches herself at him, and he catches her with a laugh, spinning her until she shrieks.

"Getting big, little fish," he says. "Soon you'll be bigger than Jack."

"I'm already cooler than Jack," Mariana says.

"That's objectively true," Baby Boy says.

"That's fair," Jack concedes.

Baby Boy grins at him over Mariana's head, and Jack's chest tightens.

Jack looks away before Baby Boy can notice him staring.

Later, when the sisters are busy and the evening air is warm and salt-sweet, Baby Boy sits beside Jack on the porch with a look Jack recognizes. The look that means he's been thinking about something for longer than he's letting on.

"I was at the dock this morning," Baby Boy says. "Pedro was talking."

"Pedro's always talking."

"No, like — talking. About pirates." Baby Boy drops his voice. "There's a crew operating out of the islands. Foreigners. They've been raiding cargo ships, reselling to buyers in Coron and Puerto. Pedro says they pulled off a big haul last week — nobody knows if it was them or the ghost ship, but the cargo vanished and someone's getting rich."

Jack is quiet. Pirates. Actual pirates, operating in the same water where their fathers disappeared.

"Pedro says they call the captain a king," Baby Boy continues.

"And?"

Baby Boy stretches out on the porch, hands behind his head, casual as anything. "And... we could join them."

Jack stares at him. "You're serious."

"We could run cargo. Help with raids. Make actual money." Baby Boy's eyes are bright with that reckless optimism Jack lost somewhere in the last ten years but Baby Boy somehow kept. "We could be pirates. Or we could keep gutting fish for twenty pesos a day until we die." Beat. "Actually, dying as a pirate sounds better than dying as a fish gutter."

Jack shakes his head. But he's almost smiling.

"You know you're allowed to have a life that isn't just keeping six girls alive, right?" Baby Boy says, and his voice is gentler now.

"Seven. Mom counts."

"Eight. I count too."

Jack looks at him — this boy who helped him survive when everything fell apart. Who makes Jack laugh even when everything is terrible.

Then the smile fades. "They go after stardust," Jack says quietly. "The same stuff that killed our fathers."

Baby Boy sits up. "That's a rumor. Pedro talks a lot. We don't have to go after stardust — we just join the crew, run cargo, make money. That's it."

"My father went out past midnight chasing that stuff. He didn't come back."

"I know. Mine too." Baby Boy meets Jack's eyes. "So — do we spend the rest of our lives afraid of the water? Or do we go find out what's actually out there?"

Jack looks at his house. His sisters. His mother at the window. The life he's built from scraps and will.

"There's a reason the fishermen don't go out past the Twin Peaks after midnight," Jack says. "You've heard the stories."

"Ghost stories." Baby Boy waves a hand. "Old men who drank too much tuba and saw shapes in the fog. Pedro says the pirates USE those stories — keeps everyone scared, keeps the water empty. It's a cover, Jack. Not ghosts."

Jack doesn't answer right away. The evening is warm. The water is calm. Somewhere a dog barks. Somewhere a mother calls her children home.

"Just cargo," Jack says slowly. "Just running jobs."

"Just cargo." Baby Boy touches Jack's shoulder, warm and solid. "I'll find out more tomorrow. Where exactly they dock. What they need."

Jack nods.

Baby Boy grins. That's all he needed.

# Chapter 5
# PARADISE

Baby Boy wakes to the sound of his grandmother singing.

It's not singing — more a low hum, the parish hymn she's hummed every morning of his life. *Salve Regina* under her breath while she cooks. Baby Boy could pick it out of any crowd of voices in the world.

He lies in bed (a thin mattress on a bamboo frame, sheets worn soft from years of washing) and listens. Through the wall, his mother moves in the kitchen. The clink of the coffee pot. The scrape of a match. The hiss of the stove catching. Through the window, El Nido is waking up: roosters first, then dogs, then the distant put-put of the first fishing boats heading out.

Marcus has been gone ten years. His mother sets four places at the table every morning — three for the living, one for faith. Baby Boy has never asked her to stop.

"Anak! Breakfast!"

He goes to the kitchen. The house is small — smaller than Jack's, but warmer somehow. Catalina has hung dried flowers from the ceiling beams and painted the walls a pale yellow that catches the morning light. There are photographs everywhere — Marcus and Catalina's wedding, Baby Boy as an infant, Marcus holding a fish bigger than his torso, grinning with his whole face. The photographs stopped ten years ago. The wall after that is bare.

He sits at the table. Lola Rosa sets rice and dried fish in front of him.

"I'm helping Uncle at the site this morning," Baby Boy says.

"You've been helping a lot lately," Catalina says.

"He needs the hands."

"And after?"

"Jack's."

"Always Jack's." She pours his coffee. Doesn't look up. But her mouth twists — amusement and sadness braided together so tight you can't tell which thread is which.

Baby Boy eats. The fish is salty and perfect. The rice is overcooked the way Lola Rosa always makes it, because she learned to cook during the war when you made rice soft enough for people with broken teeth and never unlearned it.

He kisses his mother's cheek. At the door, he pats his pocket. The bracelet is there. Woven threads, faded with age. He's carried it every day since he was eight.

He heads out.

---

The main road is already humming. Tricycles buzz past in clusters of three and four, their tinny engines cutting through the salt air, trailing exhaust that mixes with the smell of frying garlic and drying fish and someone's laundry detergent. Dogs trot between the buildings with purpose only dogs understand. Cats stretch on warm concrete. A rooster stands on someone's roof, screaming at the sun like it's personally offended.

Baby Boy walks. This is his town. He knows every cracked step, every leaning post, every dog by name.

The market is setting up along the main dock. Fishermen lay out the night's catch on wooden tables, women arrange vegetables on woven mats, children run underfoot stealing samples. The smell hits different at the market: brine and blood and green things, the particular wet sweetness of a tropical morning before the heat turns everything sour. Baby Boy moves through it the way water moves through coral, around, between, part of it without disrupting it.

"Kuya Baby Boy!" A kid from three houses down, maybe seven, holding up a fish. "Look what I caught!"

"That's a monster." Baby Boy crouches, examines the fish with serious attention. "This could feed a family for a week."

"It's only four inches long."

"Quality over quantity, brother."

The kid grins and runs off. Baby Boy watches him go and remembers holding up fish for his own father, getting the same exaggerated praise.

He keeps walking. Past the dive shop carved into the ground floor of a hotel. Behind its glass case, rows of Filipino breads: sugar-dusted buns, pillowy rolls, something with cheese baked in. The dive gear hangs from the ceiling like strange fruit. Past the bakery where Tita Maria is pulling pandesal from the oven. Baby Boy reaches for one as he passes and she smacks his hand without looking up. He takes one anyway. She doesn't stop him. She never does.

Past Father Miguel sweeping the church steps. "Good morning, Baby Boy."

"Morning, Father. God bless."

"God already did. The question is whether you'll do anything with it."

Baby Boy grins. Father Miguel has been saying this to him since he was twelve. It never gets old.

At the tricycle stop, motorized rickshaws with welded sidecars, painted every color, crammed with too many people, engines coughing blue smoke into the morning air. Baby Boy used to pump gas there for two years. Came home every night smelling like petrol, skin tinged gray. His uncle got him the construction gig. Better pay, better view.

Down where the tour boats launch, even this early, guides are prepping — checking bamboo outriggers, loading coolers, counting life vests. A two-story catamaran with bright orange outriggers sits at the end of the pier, its crew draped across the railings like they've fused with the boat itself. Baby Boy waves. They wave back. He knows them all.

Past Pedro's house. Pedro is on his porch, mending nets with two other fishermen: old hands, leathered and quiet. Baby Boy slows just enough to listen.

"Seven nights ago," Pedro is saying. "Near Snake Island. Whole sky lit up. My cousin was on the water — said the glow lasted ten minutes. Blue-white, like lightning trapped under the surface."

"Bulalakaw," one of the old fishermen murmurs.

"Don't say that word," the other says. "Don't even think it."

Pedro shakes his head. "I'm just saying what he saw."

"And I'm saying nobody goes near Snake Island. You remember Jaime. You remember Marcus." The old fisherman's hands tighten on his net. "My nephew saw something out past the Twin Peaks last month. Fog where there shouldn't be fog. Three masts in the mist, then gone." He spits. "Leave it alone. The sea takes what it takes."

Baby Boy stops walking. "Morning, Pedro."

Pedro looks up. A wariness shifts in his face, like he's been caught talking about what he shouldn't. "Morning, kid. Tell your uncle I'll bring the lumber by noon."

"Will do." Baby Boy doesn't move. "What fell near Snake Island?"

The old fishermen go quiet. Pedro glances at them, then back at Baby Boy.

"Nothing that concerns you, anak. Your father went chasing that kind of nothing and look where it got him."

Baby Boy keeps his face still.

"Nobody's going near it," Pedro continues, softer now. "Not the fishermen, not the tour boats, nobody. We all remember what happened. Let the sea keep its secrets."

Baby Boy nods. Then, casual: "I heard someone in town talking about pirates. Some crew with a king. They go near Snake Island?"

Pedro's eyes narrow. "Why?"

"Just curious."

Pedro studies him for a long moment. Then: "They dock on the far side of Cadlao. Between Helicopter Island and the

Twins. My cousin runs rice and fuel out to them." He leans forward. "But don't get ideas, anak. Those people are not your friends."

Baby Boy grins. "No ideas. Just curious."

He walks away. Pedro watches him go.

Baby Boy's mind is already working.

---

At the construction site, his uncle puts him on hauling duty. Concrete blocks, rebar, bags of cement. They're building a new guesthouse for tourists — two stories, bamboo frame, the kind of place that costs fifty pesos a night for locals and five hundred for foreigners. Baby Boy is short but strong — years of swimming and diving have built the kind of muscle that doesn't show off but doesn't quit.

During the break, he perches on a stack of lumber (legs dangling over the edge, balanced perfectly, the way he sits on everything) and looks out at the bay. From here he can see Jack's house. The stilt house with the patched roof, the porch where Jack sits every evening while the village winds down around him.

Baby Boy's chest does the thing it always does when he thinks about Jack — a fist closing gently around his heart. A pressure that's been there so long he doesn't notice it anymore.

Just the way Jack's face is the first thing he looks for in any room.

---

That afternoon, Jack's house.

Mariana launches herself at Baby Boy the moment he steps onto the porch. He catches her, spins her, sets her down. Jack is in the kitchen stirring a pot that smells like fish and exhaustion.

"You look terrible," Baby Boy says.

"Thanks."

"No, like terrible. Like 'shipwrecked on an island for forty days' terrible."

"What's your excuse?"

"I hauled concrete all afternoon and I still look better than you."

Jack glances at him. Almost smiles. "You do, actually."

The way he says it — quiet, unguarded — makes Baby Boy's heart do the fist thing again.

But Jack is already turning back to the pot, the moment gone.

Baby Boy picks up a knife and chops vegetables. Works in silence for a moment. Then, quiet enough that the sisters can't hear:

"I talked to Pedro this morning. The pirates dock on the far side of Cadlao, between Helicopter Island and the Twins. Two foreigners. A Brit and an Australian." He keeps his voice even. "And Jack — a star fell near Snake Island. Seven nights ago. Nobody will go near it. The whole town's afraid."

Jack goes still.

"Fresh stardust on the seafloor and not a single fisherman in El Nido brave enough to touch it." Baby Boy sets down the knife. "But these pirates don't have that fear. They're outsiders."

Jack doesn't say anything for a long time. The pot bubbles. Mariana laughs at something in the other room.

"Tomorrow," Jack says finally. "We go find them."

Baby Boy nods. Picks the knife back up. Goes back to chopping.

# Chapter 6
# THE ENDLESS SUMMER

Jack wakes to two of his sisters screaming about shorts.

"JACK! She took mine again!"

"Did not!"

"Did too! You're wearing them right now!"

Jack opens his eyes. Someone's foot is in his face. Mariana is using his arm as a pillow, drooling. He extricates himself — expert at untangling from sisters without waking them — and climbs down the ladder.

He catches his reflection in the small mirror by the door. Nineteen, about to turn twenty. Lean and sun-browned, wiry muscle from a decade of diving and rowing. Dark hair grown longer than his mother would like.

He flexes his arm. Grins at his reflection. Gives himself a quick wink. Still got it.

Lucia is already up, making coffee on the small propane stove. The altar beside the stove is freshly tended — sampaguita tucked beside the old carved figure. Lucia's work. Every morning.

"They're fighting about shorts again," Jack says.

Lucia pours him coffee without asking — black, no sugar. "Mariana needs her permission slip signed for the field trip to Puerto Princesa. Two hundred pesos."

Jack's stomach tightens. A day's catch, maybe two. But that's a day's catch not going to rice or the electric bill. "Okay."

"Jack —"

"I'll figure it out."

She doesn't push. Just squeezes his hand once, quick and firm, then goes back to cutting mango. There's a book open on the counter — old, water-stained, the pages yellow. Hand-drawn illustrations of plants and roots, labeled in a mix of Tagalog and something older.

"Lola Rosa gave it to me," Lucia says, noticing him looking. "It belonged to her grandmother's sister. She was a healer — knew every plant on the island." She traces an illustration. "This one. Lagundi. It says it calms the body when it's fighting itself."

"That's cool," Jack says.

Lucia almost smiles. "Go deal with the shorts."

He settles three arguments, makes breakfast for seven, braids a little one's hair, and checks on his mother — still on the porch, still staring at the water — all before nine in the morning.

Baby Boy arrives just as Jack is scraping the last of the rice porridge into bowls. Steals a piece of pandesal from the plate, drops his voice.

"I found them. Far side of Cadlao. Two foreigners, been running these waters for years."

Jack looks at the kitchen. At Mariana eating pandesal with both hands.

"Let's go."

———————————————————

They take Jack's banca out in the late afternoon — his father's banca, patched and repaired so many times it's barely the same boat. The paddle is smooth from twenty years of hands, and when Jack grips it he can feel the grooves where Jaime's fingers wore the wood thin.

They paddle through the bay as the light goes honey-gold.

Beyond the village, the islands rise. Matinloc in the distance, massive, the ruins of an old Spanish shrine on its peak.

Jack and Baby Boy paddle between the karsts, into the network of channels and passages that only locals know. The water deepens as they go, green to blue to ink. Fish dart beneath them. A reef shark patrols lazily.

"There," Baby Boy says, pointing.

Anchored in the deep channel — a sailboat. Maybe thirty feet, well-maintained, white hull, sails furled neatly. The name painted on the stern reads *Endless Summer* in fading blue letters.

On the deck, two people.

A man, tall and lean, wire-rimmed glasses catching the light, light brown hair sun-bleached and shaggy. British, Jack can tell from the pale skin turned ruddy by the sun, the careful precision of someone still adapting to the heat after years in it.

A woman — shorter, athletic, dark brown skin, natural curls pulled back in braids. She moves with easy confidence on the deck, barefoot, a wrench in one hand like she's been fixing something. When she laughs at something the man says, it's loud and real and unself-conscious.

They look up as Jack and Baby Boy approach.

Baby Boy calls out: "You King Arthur?"

The two exchange a glance.

"Depends who's asking," the man says in that clipped accent.

"We heard you run cargo." Baby Boy paddles closer. "We want in."

The woman grins. "You're just kids."

"We're nineteen and eighteen," Baby Boy says.

"Like I said." But she's still smiling. "Come aboard."

---

"Arthur Smith," the man says, extending his hand as they climb over the railing. Then, with visible pain: "Though everyone calls me King Arthur. Which I did not choose."

"He tried to break up a bar fight his first week in El Nido," Jodi says, moving toward the galley. "Waded right in — 'Gentlemen, please, let's be civilized about this' — while this massive local guy was about to kill a tourist. So polite he made everyone angrier. Ended up in the harbor, glasses still on, dignity completely gone. A fisherman yelled 'Long live the king' and it stuck."

"I was trying to be helpful," Arthur says.

Baby Boy grins. "So you're telling me your name is King Arthur, you live on a boat, and you fight crime. Are you sure you're not a children's book?"

Jack laughs. Can't help it. Arthur looks wounded. Jodi looks delighted.

"I'm Jodi," she says, pouring water into a kettle. "His better half in every measurable way."

The cabin below deck is small but efficient. Every surface covered in books and hand-drawn charts. Old texts about Philippine maritime history, hand-copied illustrations of boats and islands and creatures. Arthur's handwriting fills every margin.

Arthur settles behind the navigation table. "So. You want to run cargo."

"We want to make money," Jack says. "However that works."

"Fair enough." Arthur cleans his glasses, slow and deliberate, like he's buying time to think. "There's a merchant ship coming through in three days. Portuguese cargo — spices and textiles from Vietnam, heading to Manila. It's tight with just the two of us. Easier with four."

"If you listen," Jodi adds. "If you don't panic. People die doing this."

"Cool," Baby Boy says. "So we'll probably die."

"That's not —" Jack starts.

"No, I heard her. We'll probably die." Baby Boy grins. "I'm in."

Arthur studies them. Then nods. "Three days. Midnight. Dark clothes. Nothing that makes noise."

They talk logistics for a while — approach routes, timing, how the cargo ships run their watch rotations. Jodi draws a rough map on a napkin. Arthur explains how they fence the goods through a contact in Coron.

Jack relaxes. Baby Boy asks good questions. The four of them settle into a rhythm that surprises Jack — how easily this works.

Then a silence opens up — the kind that comes after the business is done and people are deciding whether to be honest with each other.

Arthur fills it. He gestures at the books, the charts covering the navigation table. "We've been researching these waters for years. The stories, the history. We saw the star fall. Seven nights ago, near Snake Island." He glances at Jodi. "Whatever rumors you've heard about pirates going after stardust — that's not us. We've never gone after the stuff. Never seen it up close. We run cargo."

Baby Boy leans forward. "Our fathers went after that once." His voice is quiet. "The sea took it back. And took them with it."

Arthur and Jodi go still.

"Jaime and Marcus," Arthur says slowly. "You're their sons."

Jack's head snaps up. "How do you know their names?"

"It's El Nido." Arthur shrugs. "Two fishermen disappear the same night a star falls — people talk. Everyone knows."

Jack nods.

"And you want to follow them to their graves?" Arthur's voice isn't unkind. Just honest.

"I want to understand what happened to him," Jack says.

"My father wore a piece of fallen star around his neck," Jack continues. "A glowing stone. It changed him. Made him stronger at first. Then it made him violent. Then the sea took him."

Jodi goes still. The wrench in her hands stops moving.

"That's what happened to my sister," she says quietly. "A glowing stone from a trader in Coron. She wore it around her neck. She got sick." Her jaw is tight. She reaches into her pocket and pulls out a cord with a small stone hanging from it. Dull now, barely glowing, a faint blue-white pulse like a heartbeat winding down. "This is what she was wearing. I took it off her when she couldn't anymore."

She holds it out. Jack stares at it. Small. Diamond-sized. The same color as the light that fell from the sky when he was nine.

"Is this the same thing your father wore?" Jodi asks.

Jack nods. Can't speak.

Jodi tucks it back into her pocket. "I came here to find out what it was. Arthur's been helping me research."

"That's why you're here," Jack says.

"That's why I'm here."

The silence on the boat changes.

"We don't know enough to go safely," Arthur says. "And going without knowing —"

"Is how people get hurt," Jack finishes.

"Yes."

Baby Boy looks at Jack. Jack looks back.

"So after the cargo raid," Baby Boy says, turning back to Arthur. "We go to Snake Island. Together. All four of us. You bring the research. We bring the local knowledge. Nobody goes alone."

Arthur is quiet. Jodi watches him.

"Prove yourselves on the merchant ship first," Arthur says. "Then we talk about Snake Island."

"Deal," Baby Boy says, before Jack can argue.

---

They paddle back toward El Nido as the sun sets.

"We're doing this," Baby Boy says. "Together."

Jack grins back.

"Together."

# Chapter 7
# THE FIRST RUN

The three days before the raid pass like water through a sieve.

He goes through the motions of his life with a strange double consciousness. On the surface, everything is normal: wake at dawn, make breakfast, settle arguments, check on his mother, work odd jobs around the village.

Baby Boy feels it too. Jack can tell by the way he keeps grinning for no reason, by the way he'll stop mid-sentence and just look at Jack like they're sharing the world's best secret.

"What?" Jack asks the second time he catches Baby Boy staring.

"Nothing." But his smile is huge. "We're doing it. We're actually doing it."

"We haven't done anything yet."

"We will though."

---

The night of the raid, Jack can barely eat dinner.

"You okay, Kuya?" Mariana asks, watching him push rice around his plate.

"Fine. Just tired."

Lucia looks at him across the table with those too-knowing eyes. "You look nervous."

"I'm not nervous."

"You're a terrible liar." But she doesn't push. Just holds his gaze a beat too long. "Be careful tonight. Whatever you're doing."

"I'm going fishing with Baby Boy."

"At midnight?"

"Best time for certain fish."

Lucia doesn't believe him. But she nods anyway.

After dinner, Jack prepares. Dark shirt: an old black tank top worn soft from washing. Dark shorts, navy blue, no reflective strips. He removes his watch, everything that could catch light or make noise. He checks his knife — his father's folding blade, the one Jaime left behind in the kitchen drawer. Small, sharp, reliable.

His mother is on the porch when he leaves. She doesn't look up.

"I'll be back before dawn, Mama," he says quietly.

Jack kisses the top of her head and leaves.

Baby Boy is waiting at the dock. All black: a sleeveless shirt that shows his broad shoulders, dark shorts, nothing that could give them away. His face is set with determination, but when he sees Jack his expression softens.

"If I die tonight," Baby Boy says, "tell my grandmother I died doing something cool. Not the truth."

"Ready?" Jack asks.

"No." Baby Boy grins. "Let's go anyway."

They take the banca out under cover of darkness. The moon is barely a crescent, perfect for piracy, terrible for navigation. But Jack knows these waters.

The village lights fade behind them.

The Endless Summer is anchored where they left her. Arthur and Jodi are on deck, both in dark clothes, moving with quiet efficiency. They look up as Jack and Baby Boy approach. Arthur nods.

"Good. You dressed right. Come aboard."

They tie the banca to the stern and climb over the railing. Tethered alongside the Endless Summer is a small motorboat, maybe twelve feet, open hull, an outboard engine that looks like it's been rebuilt more than once.

"That's our ride tonight," Jodi says, nodding at it. "Quiet engine, low profile, fast enough to outrun anything that chases us."

Below deck, Arthur spreads a hand-drawn chart across the navigation table. The lantern is turned low.

"The cargo ship passes through open water north of El Nido's coast around two in the morning," he says, tracing a route with his finger. "Modern vessel. Steel hull, maybe two hundred feet, containers stacked on deck. Crew of ten, most asleep. One or two on watch."

"How do we get aboard?" Baby Boy asks.

Jodi answers. "We don't. Not all of us. Arthur and I climb the hull. Grappling hooks on the railing, up the side. We know the layout. You two stay in the motorboat and take cargo when we pass it down."

"We're pack mules?" Baby Boy sounds disappointed.

"You're learning," Arthur corrects. "First rule of piracy: know your role. Don't try to be a hero." He looks at Jack. "Heroes get killed."

"I had a partner before Jodi," Arthur says quietly. "A mate from London. Ben. He tried to be a hero on our second run — swam back for a bag we'd dropped, right into the ship's propellers." He adjusts his glasses. "So when I say stay in the boat and do your job, take me literally."

The cabin goes quiet.

"Can you handle that?" Arthur asks Jack. "Staying in the boat, doing your job, not trying to save anyone?"

"Yes," Jack says.

Arthur doesn't look away. "Second rule: if it goes wrong, you scatter. Don't come back for us. Take the motorboat to the nearest cove. We'll find you there."

"That's a terrible rule," Jack says.

"That's the rule that keeps you alive." Arthur's voice is gentle but firm. "Jodi and I have been doing this for years. We know the risks. The best thing you can do if things go sideways is save yourselves."

Jodi catches Jack's eye. "Your sisters need you alive more than they need you brave. Yeah?"

"Yeah," Jack says.

---

They take the motorboat out, engine barely above idle. The small hull cuts through the water low and dark — no lights, no wake, four people moving through blackness. Jack has never been out on the water this late, this far from shore.

Baby Boy stands beside him, close enough that their arms almost touch.

"Scared?" Baby Boy asks quietly.

"Terrified."

"Yeah. Me too." His hand finds Jack's in the dark. Squeezes once. "But we've got each other, right?"

"Right."

Then Arthur says softly from the helm: "There. Two points off starboard."

Lights in the distance. The cargo ship, right on schedule. Massive: a wall of steel cutting through the dark water, containers stacked high, running lights reflecting off the surface. Bigger than anything Jack has seen up close.

"Positions," Jodi says.

Arthur cuts the engine and they drift alongside the hull. The steel rises above them, twenty, thirty feet of riveted metal, barnacles crusting the waterline, the ship's wake rocking the motorboat in slow swells.

Arthur and Jodi pull on dark gloves, check their knives, secure their bags. Arthur catches Jack's eye and nods once. *Stay in the boat.*

They're moving. Jodi swings the grappling hook twice and releases — it catches the railing with a dull clank lost under the engine noise. Arthur's follows a second later. They climb the steel side of the hull hand over hand, fast, practiced, feet bracing against rivets. Within seconds they've cleared the railing and vanished onto the deck.

Jack and Baby Boy idle in the motorboat. Waiting.

Minutes pass. The ship holds course. A cigarette glows orange where someone stands watch on the far side. Voices — distant, bored.

Then: a splash.

A waterproof bag hits the water beside the motorboat, tied with rope. Jack grabs it — heavy, full of grain or powder that shifts and settles. Worth more than his family makes in a month.

Another bag. Baby Boy catches it.

Another.

Another.

They work quickly, stacking the bags in the hull. Jack's arms burn.

Then: voices. Raised. Angry.

"— the hell are you —"

"GO!" Arthur's voice, sharp.

Jodi hits the water first, then Arthur right after, both dropping from the railing, splashing down hard. Jodi surfaces immediately, swimming for the motorboat. But Arthur — a bag snagged on the railing above, the rope tangled around his arm, pulling him half out of the water as the ship drags him forward.

He's fumbling for his knife, trying to cut the rope, the ship's momentum hauling him along the hull.

Jack doesn't think.

He pulls his father's folding knife from his belt — Jaime's old blade, small and sharp. Leans over the motorboat's side. Slashes the rope above Arthur's arm. It parts in one cut.

Arthur drops — but the ship's wake catches him and he goes under, vanishing into black water.

"ARTHUR!"

Jack dives in after him.

The water hits cold. Salt in his eyes. He kicks down through the dark toward the shape of Arthur sinking, the cargo ship's hull a wall of iron rushing past above them. He grabs Arthur's collar. Kicks hard for the surface.

They break together, gasping.

Baby Boy is at the motorboat's edge, hands out. Jodi has the engine running. The ship's lights blaze bright as someone sounds an alarm. They haul Arthur in first, then Jack — Baby Boy gripping his wrist hard enough to bruise.

They run.

The motorboat's engine opens up, louder than Jack expected, but fast. They skip across the dark water, bouncing over the cargo ship's wake, the steel wall shrinking behind them. After five minutes Jodi cuts the engine and they drift in silence between the islands.

Baby Boy catches Jack's eye and whispers: "This is the most fun I've ever had. Is that wrong?"

"Yes," Jack whispers back.

"Okay but it IS though."

Arthur turns to Jack.

"What the hell were you thinking?"

"You were stuck —"

"I was FINE. I told you. If it goes wrong, save yourself."

"You were being dragged along a cargo ship."

"I had it! I would have cut it!" Arthur runs his hands through his wet hair. "You don't dive in after a man going under propellers, mate. You don't have to save everyone."

The words land like a fist. "Yes I do."

It comes out simple. Fact.

Arthur stares at him. Then, softer: "Why?"

Jack looks back toward where El Nido sits in the dark. His house. His sisters. His mother on the porch. The answer is there. He doesn't say it.

Jodi breaks the silence. "Well. We're alive and we've got the cargo. I'd call that a win."

"Barely," Arthur mutters. But he's almost smiling. "You did well. Both of you. Mostly." He looks at Jack. "But next time, trust your team."

"I can try," Jack says.

Arthur laughs, surprised. "At least you're honest."

They motor back to the Endless Summer slowly. Baby Boy sits beside Jack on the deck, shoulders touching.

Then, quietly: "You're going to get yourself killed."

"I'm fine."

"You say that a lot. 'I'm fine.' 'It's okay.'" Baby Boy turns to look at him. "But you're not always fine, Jack. And someday you're going to try to save someone who doesn't need saving and die for it."

"Would you let me drown?" Jack asks. "If it was me stuck? Would you swim away?"

Baby Boy's jaw tightens. "That's not fair."

"Would you?"

"Of course not."

"Then don't ask me to."

They look at each other. Baby Boy opens his mouth like he wants to say something else, but Jodi calls from below.

"Boys! Help me with these bags!"

They spend the next hour sorting cargo on the Endless Summer. Spices in sealed containers: saffron, cardamom, star anise. Bolts of silk probably destined for Manila's wealthy. Several bottles of Portuguese wine that Jodi holds up to the lantern light with visible delight.

"This alone pays for a month," she says. "We'll give you boys a third. Fair?"

"More than fair," Baby Boy says.

Arthur watches Jack, thoughtful behind his glasses. "You did well tonight. Stupid, but well." He glances at Jodi, then back at the boys. "Two days. We go to Snake Island. See what fell out of the sky."

"Together," Baby Boy says.

Arthur nods. "Together."

---

They paddle home in the banca as the sky goes pale at the edges. Jack's whole body aches.

Baby Boy is quiet for a while. Then:

"We did it."

Jack huffs a tired laugh.

"This is just the beginning."

Jack grins. "Good. Let it change."

The village appears ahead, waking up, smoke rising from cooking fires. They've been out all night stealing from a cargo ship and nobody knows.

# Chapter 8
# DESCENT INTO DARKNESS

Two days pass. Jack barely sleeps.

He works. He cooks. He settles arguments about shorts and missing hairbrushes and who ate the last of the pandesal. But underneath all of it, the pull: steady, patient, a current he can feel in his chest.

Baby Boy shows up both evenings. They sit on the porch and don't talk about what's coming. Don't need to. It sits between them like a third person.

Baby Boy says on the second night, both of them watching the sunset: "You thinking about it?"

"Can't stop thinking about it."

"Scared?"

Jack considers lying. Doesn't. "Terrified."

Baby Boy grins. "Good. Me too."

They sit in comfortable silence, shoulders touching.

---

The night arrives. Moonless. Clear. The water so still it looks solid.

They paddle out to the Endless Summer in the banca. Arthur and Jodi are already geared up — wetsuits, tanks strapped, weight belts buckled. The motorboat is loaded with two more sets of gear.

"This isn't a treasure hunt," Arthur says as they transfer to the motorboat. "We collect fragments. We document what we find. We study it." He looks at both boys. "Nobody takes unnecessary risks."

Jodi hands Jack and Baby Boy their wetsuits. She checks their gear — regulators, tanks, weight belts, dive computers, waterproof lights. Goes through everything twice.

She reaches into her pocket and pulls out her sister's necklace. The stone doesn't glow anymore. But it has the same crystalline structure, the same angular shape as the fragments in Arthur's research photos.

"This is what my sister wore," Jodi says. "What made her sick. If what we find down there looks like this — that's what we're collecting. And that's what we're respecting."

She puts the necklace back in her pocket. Never near her neck.

"Biggest danger at depth is nitrogen narcosis," she says. "Some people call it rapture of the deep. You feel drunk, euphoric, like nothing can hurt you. Makes you stupid. Makes you take risks." She looks at Jack. "If you start feeling strange, seeing things, hearing things, signal immediately and we surface. Your mind will lie to you down there. Trust the gear, not the feeling."

"Got it."

"Second danger is the bends. Come up too fast, nitrogen bubbles form in your blood. Can kill you, cripple you."

She taps the dive computer. "When this says stop, you stop. You don't think about it, you don't argue, you just stop and wait."

"Clear."

"Third danger is the water guardians," Arthur adds quietly. "They haven't been seen near Snake Island, but that doesn't mean they're not watching. If you see anything — any movement, any shapes, any lights that aren't ours — you surface immediately. We're not here to be brave. We're here to collect and get out."

They motor toward Snake Island. No lights. The engine barely above idle. The island appears as a dark shape against dark sky — small, rocky, the single dead tree at its peak like a finger pointing at nothing.

Arthur cuts the engine fifty yards offshore. They drift.

"Sixty feet to the impact site," Arthur says. "Deep for a first dive but within safe range. We descend together. Slow. Follow the anchor line. Every twenty feet we stop and equalize — clear your ears, let your body adjust. At forty we stop for a full minute. Then we're at the bottom."

"How long down there?"

"Ten minutes. Maybe twelve. That's it. Any longer and we won't have enough air for the safety stops on the way up." His face is serious in the dim light. "Work fast. Collect what you can. Don't get greedy."

"What are we looking for exactly?" Baby Boy asks.

"Fragments," Jodi says. "Pieces of the star embedded in coral, in rock, in sand. They'll be glowing — faint blue-white light. Like stars underwater." She touches her pocket where the necklace sits. "You'll know them when you see them."

Jack sits on the gunwale in his wetsuit, tank strapped to his back. His heart hammers against his ribs.

Baby Boy sits beside him, close enough that their knees touch. Bouncing his leg, adjusting his mask, eyes too bright.

"You ready?" Baby Boy asks.

"No."

"Yeah. Me neither." But Baby Boy is grinning — that wild fierce grin that means he's about to do something reckless and doesn't care. "Let's do it anyway."

"Masks on," Arthur says.

They roll backward off the motorboat. The water closes over Jack's head — warm, dark, immediate. His regulator hisses. Bubbles climb past his mask. The dive light on his wrist cuts a pale cone through the black.

They descend.

---

The world changes at twenty feet.

The moonlight from the surface — what little there is — fades to almost nothing. Jack's dive light becomes the only reality. Everything beyond its reach is black. The kind of darkness that pushes against you.

His ears equalize with a series of pops. The pressure builds — sinuses, chest, behind his eyes. Jodi signals: *okay?* Jack gives the thumbs-up even though okay isn't exactly the word.

At thirty feet, the coral begins. Brain coral in massive mounds. Staghorn forests reaching upward like skeletal hands. Sea fans waving gently in the current. A school of fish swims past, hundreds of silver bodies moving as one, and Jack's breath catches at the beauty of it.

At forty feet, Arthur signals: one minute stop. They hang on the anchor line, suspended in blue twilight. The cold begins to bite, seeping through the wetsuit. Jack's ears pop again. He pinches his nose, blows gently. Baby Boy does the same beside him. Their eyes meet through masks. *You okay?* Jack nods.

He looks down. Below them: darkness that suggests vast spaces.

Arthur signals: continue.

The last twenty feet are the hardest.

The water is indigo, nearly black. Jack's dive light penetrates a few feet before the darkness swallows it. The temperature has dropped hard. Hands going numb despite the gloves. His breathing sounds different down here. Louder. More labored. Like the water itself is pressing against his lungs.

A lightness in his head. A strange euphoria creeping in at the edges. Everything unreal. He has to focus to remember where he is.

Nitrogen narcosis.

Then he hears it.

Faint. At the edge of hearing — or maybe below hearing, felt rather than heard. A sound like singing, but not any singing he recognizes. No melody. No words. Just a vibration in the water that passes through his body.

He turns. Nothing behind him but black water and coral.

Lights. At the corner of his vision — small, moving, blue-green. When he turns his head to look directly at them, they're gone. Only the darkness.

He shakes his head, trying to clear it, and focuses on Baby Boy's silhouette ahead.

Then Arthur's light sweeps across something and stops.

The crater.

---

It's smaller than Jack expected but no less extraordinary. A circular depression in the seafloor, maybe thirty feet across — sand unnaturally white, burned clean by impact. Jack knows coral. He's dived reefs his whole life.

This isn't that.

The coral has grown fast here, years of growth in what should have taken decades, and it's grown strange. It reaches inward instead of up, wrapping around the embedded fragments. Like the ocean tried to hold what fell here. Protect it. Consume it.

And embedded in that strange coral, in the sand, in the crevices between rock —

Light.

Blue-white fragments glowing against the dark seafloor, pulsing faintly with their own rhythm. Dozens of them. Diamond-sized. Scattered like seeds.

Jack forgets to breathe.

Arthur signals: *spread out, ten minutes.*

He demonstrates the hand signal — open palm, fingers spread, then both hands showing ten. They separate.

Jack heads for a cluster of rocks on the far side where several fragments are embedded. He pulls out the chisel Arthur gave him and starts working carefully, trying to pry a fragment free without shattering it.

Harder than he expected. The fragments are fused deep, not sitting on the coral but woven through it, as though the coral grew around them the way a body grows around a splinter. His fingers are clumsy with cold and the narcosis makes everything feel off. He chips away carefully, his light casting strange shadows, and the first fragment comes free.

Small. The size of a rough-cut diamond. Angular, crystalline, silver-white. It pulses in his hand like a heartbeat. Warm despite the freezing water.

The moment his fingers close around it, his whole body jolts — a shock, electric and deep, shooting up his arm and into his chest. He drops it. It tumbles into the sand, still glowing.

Jack stares at his hand. Tingling. Pulse racing.

He reaches again. This time he's ready — the shock doesn't come. Instead: warmth. Spreading from his palm up his wrist, settling into his chest. The fragment pulses against his skin and he can feel it syncing with his heartbeat, or something deeper.

He stares at the fragment in his palm.

He should put it back. Should drop it, swim away, surface, go home to his sisters and his safe small life.

He puts it in his collection bag and reaches for another.

The singing comes again — fainter now. And the lights, dancing at the edges of his vision. He keeps his head down. Doesn't look.

Baby Boy finds him five minutes later.

Jack is working on a stubborn fragment, chipping at the coral around it, when he feels a hand on his shoulder. He turns — Baby Boy, bag already half-full, eyes bright behind the mask.

Baby Boy points to Jack's bag. *How many?*

Jack shows him: three fragments, each glowing faintly through the waterproof material.

Baby Boy grins. Thumbs up.

Then — fast, almost too fast to catch — he works one more fragment loose from the sand and slips it into his wetsuit instead of the bag. Through the narcosis Jack barely registers it. He lets it go.

He reaches for the same fragment Jack is working on, both of them chipping at different sides. Their hands are close, almost touching, working in tandem. The fragment breaks free and they both reach for it at the same moment.

Their hands collide.

Close around the fragment together.

And everything stops.

Jack looks up and Baby Boy is right there, inches away, their hands wrapped around the glowing fragment between them. The pulse moves through the stone, through their fingers, through their arms, into their chests. Jack feels Baby Boy's heartbeat through the fragment. Feels it sync with his own: two rhythms finding each other, locking together, beating as one.

The water around them warms. Every fragment in the crater pulses in unison for one long moment, like the whole seafloor is breathing.

And even through the masks, even through the cold and the dark and the narcosis, Jack can see Baby Boy's eyes clearly. The gold flecks catching the dive light like sparks. Locked on Jack's face. Holding a question that has nothing to do with stardust or diving or piracy.

The moment stretches, suspended in deep water. Jack's heart hammers from the depth, from the nitrogen, from the way Baby Boy is looking at him.

Jack's hand twitches toward his regulator. Wanting to rip it out. Wanting to speak even though the words would drown.

Then it fades. The light dims. The water cools. Their heartbeats separate.

Baby Boy holds Jack's gaze. Then slowly, deliberately, he holds a finger up to his regulator.

*Shhh.*

He takes the fragment — snaps it cleanly against the coral edge. Two pieces. Diamond-sized. He tucks one under the sleeve of Jack's wetsuit, presses it flat against his wrist. Tucks the other under his own.

Jack's skin burns where the fragment touches it — a gentle, awake kind of burn.

Baby Boy squeezes Jack's hand once. The squeeze has nothing to do with the dive.

Jack squeezes back.

Baby Boy's eyes crinkle at the corners. Smiling behind the mask.

He taps his dive computer: *Time to go.*

---

The ascent is even slower than the descent: agonizing stops every twenty feet, hanging on the anchor line while their bodies off-gas nitrogen, while Jack's mind races with everything that just happened.

At forty feet they stop for three minutes. Baby Boy's hand finds Jack's in the dim blue water. Squeezes. Doesn't let go.

Jack squeezes back.

At thirty feet they stop for five minutes. The boat looms above, Arthur and Jodi's silhouettes waiting. The water is warmer here, brighter, and the narcosis has faded, leaving Jack's mind clearer but his emotions rawer.

Baby Boy is still holding Jack's hand.

At fifteen feet, the final stop — eight minutes of decompression, of watching light filter down from above, of breathing slowly and trying not to think about what happens when they surface.

Arthur signals: surface.

They break through into warm night air. Jack rips off his mask and breathes deep — salt and freedom.

"Jack. JACK." Baby Boy is grinning so wide it splits his face. "We did it."

"We almost drowned."

"Yes but we're ALIVE which is the best part."

Jack laughs — can't help it — bright and young and free.

Arthur and Jodi help them aboard. The fragments spill onto the deck, still glowing, still pulsing. Eleven pieces total in the collection bag.

"Bloody hell," Arthur breathes, studying them under the lantern. "That's a solid haul."

Jodi pulls her sister's necklace from her pocket and holds one of the fragments beside it. The resemblance is unmistakable.

"Same thing," she says quietly. "The same thing that made my sister sick."

Nobody speaks for a moment.

"We study these," Arthur says. "Carefully. Document everything — weight, light patterns, how they respond to proximity. This is research, not treasure."

---

They motor back slowly — four tired people in a boat full of stolen starlight. Baby Boy sits close to Jack, their shoulders pressed together, and neither of them mentions the moment underwater.

Jack stares at the fragments in the bag. Eleven diamond-sized pieces. Each one pulsing faintly.

Under his wetsuit sleeve, pressed flat against his wrist, the twelfth fragment pulses warm. Baby Boy's is doing the same. Jack can see the faint glow through the neoprene at his wrist.

Their secret. Taken before the count. Hidden against skin.

They catch each other's eyes.

*I know.*

*Me too.*

They look away before Arthur notices.

They transfer to the banca for the paddle home. Arthur and Jodi wave them off — "Rest today. Let your bodies clear the nitrogen. Then we plan."

They paddle in silence until the Endless Summer is a speck behind them.

Baby Boy peels back his wetsuit sleeve. The fragment glows faintly against his wrist. He works it free and holds it in his palm. Jack does the same.

"No one can know," Baby Boy says.

"I know."

"Not Arthur. Not Jodi. Not your sisters. Not my grandmother."

"I know."

"We keep them in our pockets. Hidden. Always."

Jack nods. The fragment pulses against his palm and warmth moves through him — the warmth of Baby Boy's hand in the dark water.

He wraps the fragment in a scrap of cloth and puts it in his pocket. Baby Boy does the same.

"Did you hear it?" Jack asks. "Down there. The singing."

Baby Boy doesn't answer right away. He's looking at the water — not at the surface but into it.

"Yeah," he says. Quiet. Too quiet. "I heard it."

"What did it sound like to you?"

Baby Boy's hand goes to his chest. Presses flat against his sternum, an unconscious gesture, like he's checking for a pulse. Then he catches himself and drops the hand.

"Nothing," he says. "Probably the nitrogen." He grins. But the grin is wrong. Too fast. The kind of grin Baby Boy uses when something scares him and he doesn't want Jack to know.

They paddle home as dawn breaks. Jack transfers the fragment to his dry clothes on the dock. When he closes his hand around it, he can feel it, faint, like an echo: Baby Boy's heartbeat.

He keeps it.

———

Later that day, after Jack has slept a few hours, he goes to the porch where his mother sits.

"Mama," he says quietly. "I found work. Good work. We'll have more money soon."

She doesn't respond.

Jack kneels beside her chair and takes her hand.

"I'm going to fix things," he says.

No response.

But as he stands to leave, his mother's hand tightens on his. Just for a moment. Just enough to say: *I hear you. I'm still in here.*

More than she's given him in months.

———

That night, he and Baby Boy meet on the porch after the sisters are asleep.

Baby Boy says: "I helped my uncle move materials today. Carried twice what I normally could. He didn't notice. But I did."

"Felt good?"

"Felt like I could actually make a difference." He pauses. "I keep reaching for it. In my pocket. To feel it's there."

"Me too," Jack says.

They sit with that truth between them.

Baby Boy's hand finds Jack's in the darkness. "We'll watch each other. Make sure neither of us loses ourselves."

"Promise?"

Jack looks at him.

"Promise," Jack says.

# Chapter 9
# THE CORD

Baby Boy wakes to the kitchen sounds — the wet hiss of rice porridge, the morning settling into its shape.

Then Catalina calls from the kitchen: "Breakfast, anak."

He gets up.

———

At the table, Catalina watches him eat. She does this — has always done this — with a quiet attention that misses nothing. Baby Boy shovels rice porridge and fried fish and ignores the watching.

"You're stronger," she says. Not a question. "Your uncle says you're lifting twice what the other men can."

Baby Boy stares at his rice. "I've been working out."

"Mmm."

He finishes breakfast. Kisses her cheek. Heads out into the heat.

———

The construction site is loud. His uncle has three other men on the crew — older, barrel-chested, the kind who've been hauling since before Baby Boy was born. They work in easy silence, passing blocks down a line.

Baby Boy takes the end position. The heaviest lifting. Before the fragment, this spot left him shaking by noon. Now he barely notices the weight.

The other men notice. They don't say anything directly, but Baby Boy catches the glances. Tito Romy watching him hoist a bag of cement one-handed. His uncle's eyes narrowing when Baby Boy runs from the truck to the site carrying twice what he should, not breathing hard.

*They're going to figure it out.*

---

During the break, Baby Boy sits on the lumber stack, legs dangling. The bay stretches below — wide and bright, bancas in the shallows, the limestone cliffs beyond.

He reaches into his pocket. Touches the fragment through the cloth.

The warmth comes. It always comes. And with it — a presence. The echo of a heartbeat that isn't his.

*What if I stopped hiding it?*

He doesn't mean the fragment. He means the thing the fragment is a stand-in for.

Baby Boy unwraps the fragment. It sits in his palm — small as a rough-cut diamond, pulsing blue-white, warm. He looks at it for a long time.

Then he goes to the scrap pile and finds a thin leather cord — an offcut from a railing tie, something nobody will miss.

He threads the fragment onto the cord. Holds it up. The light catches the sun and throws a tiny blue flare across his hand.

He ties it around his neck.

The fragment settles against his chest, just below the collarbones, and the warmth spreads — different from the pocket. Deeper. He can feel it with every heartbeat now.

*I'm done hiding.*

He buttons his shirt over it. The glow is faint, almost invisible. But not quite.

---

After work, the bucket shower. Bamboo stall behind the house, a barrel of water, the blue plastic bucket. No tap. No warm. Scoop and pour.

He dumps the first bucket over his head.

Cold. His skin prickles, his lungs seize. But the fragment stays warm against his chest — ice water and starfire, his body caught between two temperatures. He dumps another bucket. Another. The salt and sweat and concrete dust sluice off.

He dresses. Reaches for the blue shirt — the good one. Catches himself choosing it and stops.

*You're dressing up for him. You know that, right?*

He wears it anyway. Checks his reflection in the small cracked mirror. Flexes. Grins at himself. "Devastating," he says to nobody. "Absolutely devastating."

Lola Rosa is on the porch when he comes out. Shelling peas, wrinkled hands working with the muscle memory of sixty years. She doesn't look up when Baby Boy sits beside her.

Then she does.

Her hands stop. The pea pod drops into the bowl. Her eyes fix on his chest — on the faint glow visible through the blue fabric where the shirt is thin.

She makes a sound. Small, sharp — like she's been stung. Her hand goes to her mouth.

"Lola —"

"Take it off." Her voice is shaking. "Take it off right now."

"It's just a —"

"I know what it is." She grabs his arm. Her grip is stronger than it should be, her fingers digging in. "Your father had one — on his wrist. Wrapped in cloth. He was careful." Her eyes are wet. "But Jaime — Jack's father — Jaime wore his around his neck. I watched it change him. Watched him get stronger, faster. Watched him need it. Watched him wear it closer and closer until it was part of his skin and he couldn't take it off."

Baby Boy goes still. He's never heard her talk about either of them this way.

"Your father didn't go as far," Lola Rosa says, quieter now. "He kept his wrapped. Said it helped him fish. Said it made him strong. But it was beginning to pull on him."

She picks up the pea pod with trembling hands. "The stone wants closer. Always closer. That's the trick of it."

"Lola, I'm being careful —"

"Your father said that too." She looks at him — really looks. "The women in our family were always drawn to the water. My grandmother could hold her breath longer than any fisherman in the village. People thought it was a trick." She touches his cheek. "It wasn't a trick, anak. And what you're carrying around your neck is not a stone."

Baby Boy's throat tightens.

"Be careful with what you carry close to your heart," she says. Picks up the peas again. Shells. Her hands are shaking.

She won't say more. Baby Boy knows better than to push.

He sits with her until the peas are done. Neither talks. The bay turns gold. Dogs bark. Children shout. El Nido settles into the hum of early evening.

---

That night, Baby Boy sits on the porch alone.

He touches the fragment through his shirt. The warmth is constant now, on the cord against his skin. A presence. Like wearing a heartbeat against his own.

Tomorrow Jack will see it.

Baby Boy goes inside.

His mother is doing dishes. The kitchen is warm — cooking oil and garlic and the sweetness of rice just finished. Lola Rosa sits in the corner, eyes closed.

"Goodnight, Mama."

"Goodnight, anak." Catalina dries her hands. Turns. She studies him — not the cord at his collar, just him. The whole shape of him in the doorway.

"You're different tonight."

"Mama —"

"I've been watching you love that boy since you were small."

The kitchen goes quiet.

"You think a mother doesn't notice?" Catalina's eyes are wet but she's smiling. "The way you light up when he walks into a room. The way you've been carrying a bracelet you wove for him and never had the courage to give him."

Baby Boy's hand goes to his pocket. The bracelet is there — has always been there. Woven threads, faded with age, made with clumsy fingers over three afternoons on this porch.

"How did you —"

"Because I watched you make it. Weaving and unweaving because it wasn't perfect enough." She touches his face. "You're my son. I see everything."

Baby Boy opens his mouth. Closes it.

"I keep waiting for him to be ready," he says. His voice cracks.

Catalina pulls him close. He's almost her height now — when did that happen? — but in her arms he's still the kid who crawled into her bed when the thunder was too loud.

"He'll figure it out," she says.

Baby Boy holds his mother in the warm kitchen with the garlic and the rice, and thinks: *Tomorrow. I'll give him the bracelet and say the words and stop waiting.*

---

He's almost asleep when he hears it.

Not Lola Rosa — he knows the shape of her singing, the way it moves through the walls like warm water. This is underneath the night. Low and far away, coming from the direction of the bay, and it doesn't sound like music exactly.

Baby Boy lies still. The fragment against his chest pulses once — a slow, deep throb, like a heartbeat answering a heartbeat.

The sound pulls at his sternum. Like something in the water knows he's here and is reaching for him through the dark.

He sits up. His feet touch the floor. He's standing before he decides to stand, moving toward the window before he decides to move. The bay is black glass. Nothing out there. Nothing he can see.

But the sound keeps going. Patient. Steady.

He stands at the window for a long time. His hand on the sill.

Then it stops.

Just — stops. Like someone deciding *not yet.*

Baby Boy stands in the silence for another minute. Two.

He goes back to bed. Lies down. Stares at the ceiling.

In the morning his feet are dirty and he doesn't remember walking outside. The fragment is warm against his chest, and the bay is bright and still, and the sound is gone.

He doesn't tell anyone.

# Chapter 10
# THE STARDUST PIRATES

Arthur has been studying the fragments for a week.

Jack finds him on the Endless Summer, hunched over the navigation table in the lamplight, the eleven fragments laid out in a grid on a towel. Notebooks everywhere. Sketches. Measurements. Jodi's sister's dead stone next to the living ones for comparison.

"Watch this," Arthur says. He picks up a fragment with tongs — holds it at arm's length. The glow is faint. Barely visible. He brings it closer to his chest. The glow brightens. Pulls it away. Dims. Closer. Brighter. Away. Dimmer.

"Proximity-based," Arthur says. "The closer to the body, the stronger the effect." He sets the fragment down. "Jodi's sister wore hers on a cord against her skin. Chest-level." He looks at Jack over his glasses. "That's why she got sick."

He picks up Jodi's dead stone. "This one burned out. Gave everything it had and went dark. The living ones." He gestures at the grid. "They pulse. They respond to body heat, to heartbeat. They're not rocks, Jack. They're organs. Pieces of something that was once alive."

"Pieces of something alive," Jack says.

"Pieces of something." Arthur sets the dead stone down. "We keep these wrapped. Never against skin. The power is useful at a distance — strength, speed, sharpened senses. But against the body? Against the chest?" He shakes his head. "That's what killed Jodi's sister. The closer and the longer, the worse it gets."

Jack nods. Doesn't mention the fragment pressed against his thigh through thin cotton. Doesn't mention how warm it is. How good it feels.

---

The next morning, Baby Boy arrives at Jack's house wearing the cord.

Jack sees it immediately — the thin leather against brown skin, the faint blue-white glow through the open collar of his shirt. The fragment sitting just below his collarbones like a pendant.

Jack's stomach drops.

"What is that?"

"What does it look like?" Baby Boy touches it — and his eyes half-close for a moment, shoulders dropping, before he catches himself. "It's easier to carry this way."

"Arthur said never against your skin —"

"Arthur also said not to go back for drowning people and you did that the first night." Baby Boy grins. "Stop looking at me like that."

"Like what?"

"Like you're worried."

"I'm always worried."

"I know. It's annoying. Also kind of sweet. Mostly annoying."

But Jack can't stop looking. The cord. The fragment against Baby Boy's skin.

Baby Boy sees his face. The grin softens. "I know what you're thinking. And I'm not him. Okay?"

"Okay."

"Then trust me."

In his pocket, Jack's own fragment pulses warm. He wraps his hand around it — a habit now, automatic — and Baby Boy's heartbeat is there. Strong and steady through the cloth, the same rhythm that synced with his in the dark water sixty feet down.

———————————————

The raids get easier after that. Nothing about stealing from cargo ships in the dark is ever easy, but easier. Jack can hold his breath longer now, swim faster, haul weight that would have floored him a month ago.

Baby Boy changes too, but differently. Where Jack becomes more controlled, Baby Boy becomes bolder. First one in the water, last to leave, always pushing for one more bag.

"Now you're the one who's going to get yourself killed," Jack says after their third raid, watching Baby Boy haul himself into the motorboat laughing despite nearly getting caught by a searchlight.

"But I didn't," Baby Boy grins, water streaming off him. "Because I'm fast now. We both are."

And the money — the money changes everything.

Mariana gets her field trip. The twins get school uniforms that fit. There's meat with dinner three nights a week. Lucia stops working double shifts. Jack watches his sisters' faces when there's food on the table, when they can be children instead of tiny adults rationing rice.

By their sixth raid, people are talking.

"Did you hear about the pirates?"

"They hit three ships in two weeks—"

"Took everything and vanished like ghosts—"

"They say there's four of them. Foreign couple and two local boys—"

"No, I heard it's just some orphans, a couple of lost boys. Brothers—"

"—call themselves the Stardust Pirates—"

Jack hears the rumors in the market, at the docks, in the shops where he buys rice and fish sauce. Someone said it once and it stuck.

Baby Boy loves it. "We're famous," he says, grinning at Jack across the porch where they're helping Lucia fold laundry. "People are telling stories about us."

"Famous means noticed," Jack says. "Noticed means caught."

"Famous means respected." Baby Boy snaps a sheet — the stardust strength making the fabric crack like a whip. Lucia flinches. "Famous means people know we're not —"

"We're exactly thieves."

"We're heroes who happen to steal."

"Robin Hood is fiction."

"So were the Stardust Pirates, until we made them real."

Lucia watches without speaking. But Jack catches her looking at Baby Boy's hands — the way they grip the sheet too hard, the fabric straining — before she turns back to the laundry.

# Chapter 11
# HAND IN THE WATER

Pedro Reyes comes to the house on a Thursday.

Jack knows Pedro — everyone in El Nido knows Pedro. A fisherman. Broad-shouldered, sun-darkened, the kind of man who measures his life in catch weight. He's been fishing these waters for thirty years.

Today he looks wrong. Shaken, not sick. His hands are clenched, the way a man's hands clench when he's trying not to show fear.

"I need to talk to you," Pedro says. He glances at Baby Boy on the porch. "Both of you."

Jack steps outside. Baby Boy stands up from the railing.

"The stone," Pedro says. "The one I bought. It's gone."

Jack's voice drops. "Pedro. Where did you get a stone?"

Pedro looks away. "Doesn't matter where —"

"It matters." Jack steps closer. "Where?"

Pedro's jaw works. He doesn't answer.

"Something took it," he says instead. He's looking at the water. "I was pulling nets. Quarter mile out, past the shallows. The stone was on a cord around my wrist — wore it for weeks. Good for fishing. Made me strong enough to haul the deep nets alone."

He stops. Swallows.

"Something pulled it. From underneath. Not the current — I know current. This had direction. The cord snapped and the stone went straight down. I dove after it. Ten feet, fifteen. And I saw —" He stops again. His hands are shaking now. "I saw a hand. In the water below me. Pale. Not human. It was holding my stone and it was looking at me."

The porch goes quiet.

"I need another one," Pedro says. "Not for the strength. For protection. If they're out there — if they're watching the fishermen —"

"We don't have any," Jack says. His voice is flat.

Pedro looks at the porch boards. Pulls in a breath. "I'll pay double. Whatever Baby Boy charged me before."

"Before," Jack repeats.

Baby Boy closes his eyes. Opens them. Meets Jack's gaze.

"I sold him one," Baby Boy says. "After the dive. I took an extra and sold it to him."

"When?"

"A few weeks ago."

"A few weeks." Jack's jaw tightens. "You've been selling stardust and you didn't tell me."

"It was one fragment. Pedro needed help with his nets —"

"You LIED to me."

"I didn't lie. I didn't —"

"That's lying."

Pedro looks between them. "I didn't mean to cause —"

"Go home, Pedro," Jack says. "We can't help you."

Pedro leaves. His footsteps fade down the wooden walkway.

Jack and Baby Boy stand on the porch. The bay is calm.

"I was trying to help," Baby Boy says quietly.

"You were trying to make money. Same as our fathers."

The words hit harder than Jack intended. Baby Boy's face goes blank.

"That's not fair," Baby Boy says.

"You sold one of those things to a fisherman and the hand in the water took it back. What part of that is fair?"

Baby Boy doesn't answer. Looks at the cord around his neck. Touches the fragment.

Baby Boy's head turns toward the water. Slow, reflexive. His eyes go unfocused, his lips parting, his hand gripping the fragment now instead of touching it.

"Baby Boy."

Nothing. He's staring at the bay. His head tilted the way a dog tilts when it hears a frequency beyond human range.

"Baby Boy."

He blinks. Comes back. Looks at Jack like he forgot he was there.

"What?" Baby Boy says.

"Where did you just go?"

"Nowhere." Baby Boy drops his hand from the cord. "I should have told you," he says.

"Yeah."

"I'm sorry."

"Yeah."

They stand there.

---

The next morning, Baby Boy arrives early. Normal. Except that Mariana runs up to him the way she always does — arms out, full speed, total trust.

Baby Boy sidesteps. Clean, fast, almost without thinking.

Mariana stumbles. Catches herself. Looks up at him with huge, confused eyes.

"Not now, little fish," Baby Boy says. His voice is flat. Absent more than unkind. Like he forgot what the game was.

Lucia puts her hand on Mariana's shoulder and steers her inside without a word. But she looks back at Baby Boy, and her eyes are steady and watchful.

Baby Boy blinks. Looks at his hands. The color drains from his face.

"I didn't —" he says. "I wasn't trying to —"

"I know," Jack says.

Baby Boy leaves without saying goodbye. Jack watches him go. Lucia comes back to the porch.

She doesn't say anything about Baby Boy. She says: "I need to show you something."

# Chapter 12
# THE OLD PAGES

Lucia finds them in the back of the healer's book — the water-stained volume Lola Rosa gave her, the one with the hand-drawn plants and roots. Stuck behind the last pages, glued to the binding. She only finds them because the spine cracked last week.

The pages are old. Older than the book. Thicker paper, rougher, browned with centuries. Small cramped handwriting in a language she can't read. But the illustrations, drawn in faded brown ink between the words, those she can see clearly. Figures rising from water. A ship with crossed sails. A child with a point of light in her forehead.

And over the top of the old pages, layered like paint over paint, the handwriting of healers. Tagalog. Plant names. Remedies. Generations of women writing their knowledge over the Spanish underneath, using the pages as scrap, never knowing what was buried beneath their recipes.

She brings them to Jack.

"The spine cracked," she says. "These were underneath everything." She turns the pages carefully. Shows him the illustrations — the figures in the water, the ship, the child. "I can't read the Spanish. But look at the drawings." She pauses. "And yesterday. The way Baby Boy moved away from Mariana. The glow through his shirt. It's the same glow as these drawings."

Jack stares at the pages.

"Show Lola Rosa first," Lucia says. "She'll know what these are."

Jack nods.

---

They take the pages to Lola Rosa.

The old woman holds them in her kitchen, turning them carefully under the light. Her face changes — not surprise exactly. Recognition.

"I've seen these before," Lola Rosa says quietly. "Not these pages. But ones like them. My mother showed me when I was a girl. Pages hidden in the back of a healer's book, old Spanish writing nobody could read, with drawings of creatures in the water." She touches the illustration of the child. "We always knew they mattered. We just never knew what the Spanish words said."

"Jack knows someone," Lucia says.

Lola Rosa looks at Jack. "A researcher?"

"A friend. He reads old languages. Studies the history of these waters."

Lola Rosa is quiet for a long time. Then she stands. "Take me to him."

---

Jack brings Lola Rosa and Lucia to the Endless Summer that afternoon. Lola Rosa climbs aboard with the careful dignity of a woman who has been in boats her whole life but never one that belonged to a foreigner. She looks at the cabin — the books, the charts, the maps pinned to every surface — and her eyes narrow.

Arthur stands when she enters. He sees the pages in her hands and his eyebrows climb.

"This is Lola Rosa," Jack says. "Baby Boy's grandmother. The book belongs to her. The pages were inside it."

Arthur takes the pages carefully. Turns them over.

"Someone hid these inside a healer's book," Arthur says.

"Four hundred years of someone," Lola Rosa says. "Passed from healer to healer."

Arthur holds the pages under the lantern. His lips move as he reads — slow, halting, working through the old Spanish.

"It's a journal," he says. "A friar's journal. Dated 1578." He looks up. "This is almost five hundred years old."

"Can you read it?" Jack asks.

"Mostly. The Spanish is old but —" He's already reading again.

Baby Boy arrives and leans against the cabin doorway. He sees Lola Rosa and goes still. Turns half away from her, the way you turn from a question you can't answer yet. His hand goes to the cord at his throat. He tugs it loose under his shirt and slips the fragment into his pocket before he turns back. Lola Rosa watches him do it. Her jaw tightens but she says nothing.

Arthur translates. Haltingly at first, then faster as he finds the rhythm of the friar's voice.

"'We arrived at the northern islands on the feast of San Miguel. The captain — Diego Varga de Salazar — ordered the crew to anchor between two great limestone cliffs. The ship — the *Estrella Perdida* — lay still in water like glass.'"

Arthur glances up. "The cliffs he's describing. Those are the karsts. He's talking about here." He turns the name over once. "*Estrella Perdida*. Lost Star."

He keeps reading.

"'That first night, the water glowed. Not phosphorescence. This was focused. Pulsing. Blue-white light moving beneath the surface in patterns too deliberate to be natural.'"

Jodi leans forward.

"'At dawn, they surfaced.'" Arthur's voice changes, quieter, more careful. "'Six of them. Their lower bodies were scaled. Their upper bodies closer to human. And on their bodies: light. Not reflected. Embedded. Small points of radiance set into their skin. Alive. Pulsing.'"

Nobody speaks. The boat rocks gently. Arthur turns the page.

"'They came bearing gifts. The young one held out a shell — offered in both hands the way a child offers a drawing to a parent. Others carried coral, fish. They held these objects toward the ship with expressions I can only describe as curious. Open. Unafraid.'"

Arthur pauses. Takes off his glasses. Puts them back on.

"'I believe they were attempting to trade. I believe they thought we were like them.'"

The silence on the boat is absolute.

"Then what?" Baby Boy asks from the doorway.

Arthur reads the next passage silently first. His face changes.

"The captain saw the stones in their skin," Arthur says. He's not reading aloud anymore — paraphrasing, his voice flat. "He ordered the nets thrown. They caught the young one. A child. She didn't understand what was happening. She made a sound the friar describes as — not a scream. A question."

"Arthur," Jodi says softly.

"They pinned her to the deck. The captain knelt beside her and studied the fragment in her forehead." Arthur's voice is steady, the way voices get when the person speaking is trying not to feel what they're saying. "He cut it out."

The boat is silent except for the water against the hull.

"The others attacked. The moment the child screamed, they came at the ship from every direction. Tore the hull apart. The friar ran below. He heard —" Arthur checks the page. "'The crack of something separating from something else.'"

He sets the pages down.

"The captain held the fragment and felt power. Picked up a cargo net with one arm that normally takes three men. He wanted more. He threw the child back and ordered them to go after the large one — the mother. The one with the stone in her chest."

"What happened?" Jack asks, though he's not sure he wants to know.

"The mother sang. And the sea answered." Arthur picks up the last page. "They sank the ship. Every sailor pulled into the water. The friar survived on a piece of driftwood."

He reads the final passage aloud, slowly:

"'What we did to them was not exploration. It was not discovery. It was the same thing we have done in every land we have reached — we saw beauty, and we cut it open to see what was inside.'"

Arthur sets the page down.

"'God forgive us. They came to us with gifts.'"

---

Lola Rosa speaks first.

"They came with gifts," she says. "And the Spanish cut them open."

She's looking at the pages.

"My grandmother's grandmother was a healer," Lola Rosa says. "She knew things. About the water. About the stones that fell from the sky. About how to approach them, with offerings, with song, with permission. The way you approach anything sacred." Her hands are steady on the pages. "The Spanish came. Magellan first, 1521. He planted a cross in Cebu and a chief named Lapu-Lapu killed him for it. But they came back. They always came back."

"By the time my grandmother's grandmother was alive, the Spanish had been here for three hundred years. They'd replaced our healers with their priests. Burned our writing. Gave us their surnames from a book, a catalog, so they could count us." Her voice doesn't waver. "My family name isn't my family's name. It was assigned. And the women who knew how to live beside the sacred things in the water, the healers, the babaylan, they were called witches. Demons. They stopped practicing. Hid what they knew. Passed it in whispers."

"This is what survived," she says. She looks up at Arthur. "Until now."

Jack's hand goes to his pocket. The fragment pulses warm.

"That's why our fathers didn't know," he says. "The instructions were destroyed."

"Not destroyed," Lola Rosa says. "Hidden. Whispered. Almost lost." She looks at Lucia, standing quietly at the edge of the cabin. "Almost."

Jodi reaches into her pocket. Pulls out her sister's necklace — the cord, the dull stone. She holds it in her palm.

She puts it in the waterproof box under the navigation table.

Baby Boy watches her. His hand goes to the cord around his own neck. The fragment glowing faintly through his shirt.

He takes it off.

Holds the fragment in his palm. Puts it in his pocket.

Jack watches all of this with his hand pressed against his own pocket. He should take it out. Should put it in the box with Jodi's.

He doesn't.

# Chapter 13
# ISLAND WITH NO NAME

That evening, Arthur anchors the Endless Summer off a small island with no name. A crescent of white sand, a cluster of coconut palms, a reef in the shallows.

"We need this," Jodi says. "After that."

They swim ashore. The water is waist-deep and warm. Baby Boy is ahead, and by the time Jack reaches the beach he's dragging driftwood into a circle.

"We can't burn wood," Arthur says. "Bush fire."

Baby Boy holds up a handful of glass bottles found in the brush. Old rum bottles, beer bottles, a cracked Coke bottle. Stuffs rags in the necks, splashes lighter fluid. "Torches."

He lights them one by one. Glass-and-cloth torches stuck in the sand, flames dancing orange against the darkening sky.

"That's either brilliant or criminal," Arthur says.

"Both," Baby Boy says. "Usually both."

They sit inside the ring of fire. Jodi passes a bottle of rum. The sunset is doing something with the sky — pink bleeding into gold bleeding into violet. The cliffs across the water catch the color and throw it back.

Arthur produces a ukulele — "Don't ask where I got it" — and picks out a Filipino folk song. Baby Boy sings. His voice is rough and tuneless and completely unselfconscious. Jodi joins the chorus even though she doesn't know the words.

Jack doesn't sing. Sits with his back against a palm trunk, rum warming his chest, watching.

Watching Baby Boy. The firelight on his face. The way he throws his head back when he laughs.

He catches Jack watching. Doesn't look away. Grins.

The rum goes around again. The torches sputter in the wind. Baby Boy and Jodi scramble to relight the ones that blow out — shoving bottles deeper into the sand, cupping flames, laughing when the wind wins.

"You're going to set yourself on fire," Jack says.

"Then I'll jump in the ocean."

"The problem IS you."

"And yet you keep me around."

The wind beats them eventually. The torches gutter and die. Jodi groans. Arthur stretches out on the sand. "I'm sleeping here. Under the stars. Like a civilized person."

Baby Boy lies back too. Looks up at the sky. The stars are thick — blue and white and the faintest gold.

He pats the sand beside him. "Come on."

Jack lies down. Close enough that the length of their arms presses warm together.

The sand is warm from the day. The waves murmur against the shore.

"Jack?" Baby Boy's voice is quiet.

"Yeah?"

"This is it. Right? This is —"

He stops. Doesn't finish the word.

Jack turns his head. Baby Boy is looking at the stars. His profile sharp against the starfield. The same boy who sat under the banyan tree at eight. Close enough that Jack's chest aches.

Baby Boy's hand finds his in the sand. Warm and calloused and real.

Baby Boy's breathing slows, evens, slips toward sleep. But Jack stays awake — and a few feet down the sand, close enough to hear over the waves, Arthur and Jodi are talking, low.

Jack keeps his eyes closed. Listens.

"She'd be the same age as him," Jodi says quietly. Nodding, he can tell, toward Baby Boy. "My sister. She'd be eighteen now."

Arthur doesn't say anything. Shifts closer until his shoulder is against hers.

"I keep thinking about the friar's drawing. The child with the light in her forehead." Jodi's voice is steady but thin. "That's what the necklace looked like on my sister. A little point of light against her skin. She thought it was beautiful."

"It was beautiful."

"It was killing her." Jodi is quiet for a long time. "When this is done — when I know what it is and what it does…"

She starts to cry. Arthur holds her.

Jack lies still, eyes shut, and lets them think he's asleep.

# Chapter 14
# THE WRONG FOG

A week later, Arthur picks a target.

"One more haul," he says, charts spread on the navigation table. "Cargo ship carrying electronics. North coast. The journal doesn't pay for itself, and after that we figure out what to do with all of this."

The boys agree. Baby Boy too quickly, Jack too slowly.

That night, the four of them slip up against the cargo ship's starboard side. Arthur and Jodi go up the rope while Jack and Baby Boy wait in the motorboat. Everything runs perfectly for five minutes.

Then the fog comes — thick and grey and heavy, rolling in from the open sea against the wind. The wrong kind. Jack watches it spread across the surface and his body knows before his mind catches up.

He's seen this fog before. He was nine. Watching through window slats.

Arthur is already sliding down the rope. "Out. Now. Everyone out."

Jodi hits the water. Arthur right behind. They haul themselves into the motorboat. Arthur grabs the engine — full throttle, no stealth, just speed.

"We barely got anything —" Baby Boy says.

"We're leaving." Arthur's hands are shaking on the throttle. He's staring at the fog. Through it, just for a moment — a shape. Three masts. Tattered sails.

Then it's gone.

"Was that —" Jodi whispers.

"Don't." Arthur cuts the engine once they're clear. His breathing is ragged. "Don't say it."

They motor home in silence.

---

Back in El Nido. Just the two of them on the dock. Past midnight, the village asleep.

"We could have gotten more," Baby Boy says.

"We could have gotten killed."

"But we didn't. We can handle this —"

"You sound like my father."

The words come out harder than Jack intended. Something in Baby Boy's face closes.

"That's not fair," Baby Boy says.

"I'm worried," Jack says. "About both of us. About what this is doing."

"It's making us capable."

"That's what he said too."

Baby Boy stands. "I'm fine. You're fine."

He walks away. Jack doesn't follow.

Jack sits on the dock alone. Reaches into his pocket. The fragment is still there — warm, pulsing.

He should throw it in the water.

He wraps his hand around it and holds it tight.

# Chapter 15
# BLOOD IN THE WATER

They're still talking. Functional words. Pass the wrench. Hand me the line. What time tomorrow. But the real talking stopped after Pedro's porch, and three days haven't quelled it.

Baby Boy seems softer, though. The glow at his neck is gone — he's been carrying the fragment in his pocket since the Endless Summer. Jack catches himself noticing. Catches himself relieved.

Three days since the fog.

Three days since Jack watched it roll out of the open sea — thick and unnatural, moving against the wind, the same fog he saw through window slats when he was nine. The fog that took his father.

He sits on his porch watching the bay and thinks about the channel between Cathedral Cave and Matinloc. The stretch of water where his father disappeared ten years ago. The place nobody goes.

His father went into that water and never came back and Jack has spent ten years not knowing why. Now he's seen the same fog twice. The first time it took everything. The second time it watched him.

He needs to go.

---

He finds Baby Boy at the dock the next morning, sitting with his feet in the water, staring at the bay with that look, the one Jack's been catching for days now. Head tilted. Eyes unfocused.

"I want to go to the channel," Jack says. "Between Cathedral and Matinloc."

Baby Boy looks up. The unfocused look clears. "Why?"

"That's where they went. The night they disappeared. That's where they were heading."

Baby Boy is quiet for a moment. "You want to dive the site."

"I want to see it."

"What do you think you'll find?"

"I don't know. Something. Nothing. I need to go."

Baby Boy nods. His hand drifts to his pocket, fingers pressing against the fragment through the fabric. "Yeah," he says. "I think we should."

Jack notices the speed of the answer. Notices Baby Boy's eyes flick toward the water, the same reflex he saw on the porch three days ago.

He doesn't push.

---

They take Jack's banca. No Arthur, no Jodi, no Endless Summer. Two boys, borrowed tanks, a borrowed regulator, masks they've used since they were twelve. Jack paddles. Baby Boy sits at the bow with his back to him, facing the open water.

The silence between them isn't comfortable anymore. It used to be — used to be the best part, the way they could sit together and not need words. Now it's heavy. Full of things unsaid.

Baby Boy hums something. Stops. Hums it again. Three notes, low, repeating. He doesn't know he's doing it.

"What's that?" Jack asks.

"What's what?"

"That song. Where did you learn it?"

Baby Boy frowns. Something cracks behind his eyes. "My grandma sings it. Maybe. I don't know." He doesn't sound sure.

Jack lets it go. But he files it.

They paddle past the tourist bancas, past the kayak routes, into the channel where the limestone cliffs rise straight out of the water. Cathedral Cave on the left, Matinloc on the right. The water changes color here — turquoise giving way to deep blue where the shelf drops off.

This is where the fishermen stopped looking.

"Here?" Baby Boy asks.

Jack checks the position against what he remembers — his mother's voice, years ago, telling Lucia: *between the caves, where the water turns dark.* He nods.

They anchor. Jack stares at the water. Clear enough to see twenty feet down — white sand, scattered coral, a few fish moving through the shallows. Nothing that says *two men disappeared here.*

Baby Boy pulls on his mask. Adjusts the strap. Adjusts it again.

"You look ridiculous," Jack says.

"I always look ridiculous. It's part of my charm."

"Ready?" Jack asks. His hand is in his pocket, pressing the fragment through the cloth.

"No," Baby Boy says. Grins, the real one, quick and warm and gone before it settles. "Let's go anyway."

They roll backward into the water.

The descent is shallow. Thirty feet. Forty. Sunlight reaches the bottom. Fish school past them in bright, unconcerned clouds.

But the bottom is wrong.

Jack sees the coral first — bone-white where it should be alive. Whole patches of it dead, hollowed out, the rock around it pocked with shallow depressions where things used to be embedded. Then the floor opens. A depression in the seafloor, circular, maybe sixty feet across. The same shape as the crater at Snake Island. The same blast pattern, the same radiating cracks.

But empty.

Every crevice where stardust would have embedded: bare. The coral that grows over fragments, the bioluminescent residue, the blue-white glow — gone. Picked clean years ago — the coral has grown back over the extraction points, smooth and undisturbed, the way skin grows over old scars.

A looted graveyard.

Jack hovers above it and feels what he didn't expect: not anger, not grief. Absence. There's no marker, no memorial, no sign that two men paddled a banca over this spot ten years ago and never came home.

He signals Baby Boy: *spread out, ten minutes.* Baby Boy nods and drifts left. Jack goes right.

He searches the way you search a room after someone has moved out. Running his hands along crevices. Turning over rocks. Sifting through the silt that's accumulated in the crater's bowl, fine and white and undisturbed for years.

His fingers find something.

Small, hard, round. Buried in the silt at the crater's edge, half-wedged under a piece of dead coral.

Jack pulls it free. Brushes the sediment away.

A ring.

Gold. Thin band. Worn smooth by years of saltwater and sand, the color dulled but still unmistakable. He holds it up to the light filtering down from the surface and turns it, and on the inside, where no one would see it unless they were looking, three words engraved in a jeweler's hand:

*For forever, Joyce.*

Jack's hand closes around it. His eyes sting behind his mask. His chest seizes — not from pressure or depth but from proof. His father was here. His father's ring is here. His father took it off his finger or it was pulled from his hand or the water stripped it from a drowning man and it's been sitting in this silt for ten years waiting for his son to find it.

He puts the ring in his pocket. Next to the fragment.

---

Baby Boy has drifted far.

Jack looks up from the ring and Baby Boy is fifty feet away, near the crater's outer edge where the rock shelf drops into deeper water. He's not searching. He's floating, suspended, his body oriented toward something Jack can't see.

Then Jack sees the glow.

Faint. Barely there. One fragment they missed, small, wedged deep in a coral head at the very edge of the crater where the rock gives way to open water. A single blue-white pulse, so dim it could be mistaken for bioluminescent algae.

Baby Boy is chipping at the coral around it. His movements are frantic, wrong. His hands working at the rock like he's trying to free something trapped.

Jack signals: *Come back.*

Baby Boy doesn't respond.

Jack signals again. Louder — banging his knife handle against his tank. The sound carries through the water, sharp and metallic.

Baby Boy doesn't turn.

Jack swims toward him. Baby Boy isn't responding. Baby Boy's whole body is oriented toward that glow, leaning into it, reaching for it, his fingers scraping at the coral. Like the light is pulling him.

Jack is twenty feet away when the water changes.

---

Light.

The crater's edge erupts in bioluminescence — hundreds of points of embedded stardust flaring to life in the bodies of things Jack didn't know were there. They've been in the rock, in the coral, in the shadows of the shelf edge. Watching. Waiting. Their embedded fragments lighting up like signal fires, marking them as they peel away from their hiding places and take shape in the water.

They come from the shelf edge, from the coral formations, from the deep water beyond the crater's rim. Sleek and fast, their scales shifting color as they move, black to blue to green to violet. Their hair floats behind them like kelp. Their eyes glow silver from within. Their mouths, when they open, show rows of needle-fine teeth that catch the light like glass.

Not dozens this time.

Enough.

And they don't go for Jack.

They go for Baby Boy.

The leader comes last. Larger than the others, moving with the unhurried grace of something that has never needed to rush. The scar across her forehead, the fragment in her chest, fist-sized, pulsing so bright the water around her turns blue-white.

She swims past Jack like he isn't there. Her attention is entirely on Baby Boy. She stops three feet from him and tilts her head, studying him with an expression Jack has never seen on anything that isn't human.

She's looking at Baby Boy the way Lola Rosa looked at the fragment on his cord: with grief and love and something older than either.

Baby Boy's hands have stopped chipping at the coral. He's floating still, facing her, and his eyes behind his mask are wide but not terrified.

---

Jack moves.

He kicks hard, driving toward Baby Boy with everything the fragment gives him. The stardust hums in his blood, pushing him faster than any human should move.

A guardian intercepts. Slams into him sideways. Two hundred pounds of scaled muscle hitting him in the ribs. Jack tumbles. Gets his knife up. Slashes. The blade catches her arm and dark blood blooms in the water, but she's already circling back.

Two more cut between him and Baby Boy. Then a third. They're not trying to hurt him. They're herding him.

Jack fights. The fragment gives him strength and speed but not enough. He wounds one across the shoulder. She doesn't flinch. He kicks past another and a hand catches his ankle, claws digging in, yanking him backward so hard his mask floods.

Through the blur of saltwater he sees Baby Boy.

The guardians have him. Two holding his arms. One behind him, hands on his tank. Baby Boy thrashes —

kicking wildly, twisting against their grip, hands clawing at scaled forearms. Then his tank alarm starts shrieking — the high tinny pulse traveling through the water like a struck bell. He's burning through air, fighting too hard, his lungs already in panic.

Baby Boy's eyes find Jack's through the water.

Recognition. The same look the leader gave him. The singing told him.

His hand reaches out — fingers spread, stretching toward Jack through the water the way he reached for the fragment in the coral.

Then they take him over the edge and the dark swallows him whole.

---

Jack screams into his regulator.

Kicks after them. Dives past the shelf edge into the deeper water where the light fails. He can see the glow of them below — the bioluminescence of their embedded fragments marking their descent, getting smaller, fainter as they carry him down.

A hand grabs his tank harness from behind. Yanks him backward. He spins, knife out. But it's a guardian, and she doesn't attack. She holds him still. Her eyes glow pale silver and she looks at him with what isn't malice.

*Pity.*

She lets go. Disappears over the shelf edge after the others.

The glow fades. The water goes dark. Jack hangs in the void, sixty feet down, watching the last light of them disappear.

He doesn't follow. He can't. They're too deep, too fast. By the time he could reach them his air would be gone and he'd die in the dark and Baby Boy would still be taken and it would mean nothing.

He hangs there until his tank alarm sounds.

He kicks for the surface hard — too fast, lungs screaming, the last twenty feet a blur. Breaks the surface gasping. The channel is empty. The limestone cliffs rise on either side, indifferent. The banca rocks gently on its anchor line.

Jack drags himself aboard. Lies on the bottom of the boat trying to breathe, water streaming off him into the bilge. His chest heaves. His hands shake.

He paddles home. Each pull harder than the last. The fragment in his pocket pulsing warm against his thigh.

Baby Boy's heartbeat. Faint, but there.

If Baby Boy were dead the stone would be dead. Like Jodi's sister's.

Alive.

Arthur and Jodi are on the Endless Summer when Jack motors alongside in the banca. They see his face and stop talking.

"They took him," Jack says. "The guardians. They took Baby Boy."

Jodi's hand goes to her mouth. Arthur takes off his glasses. Puts them back on.

"How long ago?" Arthur asks.

Jack looks at his dive computer. "An hour. Maybe more."

"Where?"

"The channel. Between Cathedral and Matinloc. There's a crater there — like Snake Island but empty. They were hiding in the rock."

"We have to go," Jodi says, already reaching for gear.

"No." Arthur's voice is quiet but firm. "If they wanted him dead, he'd be dead. They took him alive. That means they want something."

"So we do nothing?"

"We plan. We figure out where they went." Arthur looks at Jack. "The leader — describe her."

"Scar across her forehead. Fragment in her chest. Big. She looked at him like she knew him."

Arthur goes still. His mouth opens, closes.

"What?" Jack demands.

"The friar's journal," Arthur says slowly. "The child the Spanish soldiers found — the one with the scar. He described where she was taken from." He moves to the navigation table. Starts pulling charts. "If the journal's coordinates are right, there's a cave system north of here. Deep. I assumed it was collapsed centuries ago, but if they've been there this whole time..."

"Can we find it?"

"Maybe. Give me a day."

"We don't have a day."

"We don't have a choice."

Jack's fist hits the table. The charts jump.

"He's alive," Arthur says. Looking at Jack with steady kindness. "I believe that. You need to believe it too."

---

They search until dark anyway. Every channel, every cove, every beach within ten miles. Arthur at the helm, grim and peeling and salt-crusted. Jodi scanning with binoculars until the light fails.

Nothing. The ocean gives back nothing.

"We've checked everything," Jodi says gently. "Arthur. We need to rest."

"One more pass." Quieter: "He's one of ours."

When they finally motor back, the village lights are on. Children playing. Families finishing dinner.

Jack sits at the bow. His hand finds the ring in his pocket. The fragment. The warmth comes, and with it, Baby Boy's heartbeat. Faint but there. Still alive somewhere in the dark.

*I love him.*

He's loved him for years and didn't know it.

*I love him and I never said it and now he's gone.*

He grips the fragment tighter. Baby Boy's heartbeat pulses against his palm.

*Hold on. I'm coming.*

---

Baby Boy's mother is on her porch. Standing at the railing, looking at the water, the way she's been standing there since her son didn't come home for dinner. Since the sun went down and the dock stayed empty. Since the knowing started in her chest.

Her eyes find Jack as he climbs out of the boat.

Her face doesn't crumble. It empties. Everything behind her eyes (the hope, the denial, the desperate bargaining) drains out of her in a single breath and what's left is a woman standing on a porch in the dark holding the railing because if she lets go she'll fall and she might never get up.

Lola Rosa catches her from behind. Holds her upright. Her face is stone but her hands are shaking.

Jack stands on the dock and can't speak. Can't look at Catalina's face and can't look away.

"Find him," Catalina says. Her voice is steady. Impossibly steady. The steadiness of a woman who has already survived one man disappearing into the water and knows exactly what this costs and is choosing to stand anyway. "You find him and you bring him home."

"I will."

"Promise me."

"I promise."

She nods once. Goes inside. The door closes. Through the thin walls, Jack hears her collapse. The sound she makes isn't a scream. It's lower, older.

Lola Rosa follows her in.

Jack walks to the end of the longest dock. Sits with his legs over the edge. The same water that took his father. The same water that took Baby Boy.

In his pocket: his father's ring, and the fragment that carries Baby Boy's heartbeat.

He sits there as the stars come out. The bay goes dark. Behind him, footsteps. He doesn't turn.

"Anak." His mother's voice. The first time she's called him that in years. "Come home."

"I can't."

"You can." Her hand on his shoulder, thin, uncertain, but there. "He'd want you home. Not here."

Jack turns. Joyce's face is still hollow, still worn. But her eyes are focused. Actually seeing him. Like she woke up when she heard Catalina's sound through the wall, the sound of another mother losing a son to the water, and recognized it as her own.

"I lost him, Mama."

"Then find him." She pulls him to his feet. Her grip is stronger than it should be. "But come home first. Your sisters need you. I need you." She pauses. "I'm sorry I haven't said that in a long time."

Jack reaches into his pocket. The fragment is there. The ring is there.

He takes out the ring. Holds it up to her in the dark.

Joyce makes a small sound — not a word.

"He didn't come back," Jack says. "But this did."

She takes it from his palm. Closes her fingers around it. Holds it to her mouth a long moment. Then she nods once, like she's been waiting ten years for it.

She slides it onto her finger beside her own.

Jack follows his mother home.

In bed, tangled with his sisters who sense the wrongness and hold him tight, Jack presses the fragment against his chest and feels Baby Boy's heartbeat: steady, distant, alive.

*I'm coming for you. I don't care how deep. I don't care what it costs.*

*I promise.*

He doesn't sleep.

# Chapter 16
# THE QUEEN'S BARGAIN

The first thing Baby Boy thinks when the guardians drag him deeper is: *Jack's going to be so mad at me.*

But it's what his brain latches onto as strong hands grip his arms, his legs, his tank, pulling him down and away from the anchor line, away from the surface, away from air and light and Jack's desperate reaching hand.

*Jack's going to try to save me and get himself killed.*

Baby Boy thrashes, tries to kick free, but there are too many of them — three, four, maybe five guardians pulling him in different directions, and even with the fragment's warmth against his skin he's no match for beings who were born to this water, who move through it the way he moves through air.

His regulator is still in his mouth. He forces himself to breathe slowly. To think.

*Okay. They're not killing me. If they wanted me dead, I'd be dead already. So they want something. Which means there's time.*

The water darkens as they descend past two hundred feet, then two-fifty — depths Baby Boy has never reached, depths that should require special equipment and decompression stops he won't get. The pressure builds in his ears until they pop painfully, and still they go deeper.

His dive computer is screaming warnings he can't hear but can see flashing red. Past the recreational limit. Past the technical limit. Past where nitrogen narcosis should make him stupid and careless.

But the fragment in his pocket keeps him sharp — warmth radiating through the wetsuit, pressing against his hip like a second pulse. Keeps his mind clear even as everything else says he should be dying.

*Silver lining,* he thinks. *The magic rocks are good for something.*

And then — faint, far away, beneath the hiss of his regulator and the rush of water — the singing.

He heard it at the crater. During the dive with Jack. That sound between hearing and feeling, the vibration that passed through his body like light through glass. He'd told Jack it was nothing. Told Jack it was the nitrogen.

It wasn't the nitrogen.

Down here, deeper than he's ever been, the sound is clearer. Not louder — focused. Like it's been waiting for him to get close enough to hear properly. A low, steady resonance that settles in his chest and stays there. In his ribs. In the space behind his sternum where his heart beats.

They swim through a kelp forest, fronds reaching tall from the seafloor far below, and Baby Boy catches glimpses of the guardians around him. They're beautiful in a way that makes his stomach clench. Something older than human.

Their scales catch what little light penetrates this deep —
black bleeding into blue, green shimmering into purple.
Their hair floats around them in strands of emerald and
silver and deep kelp-black. Their faces are almost human.
But their eyes glow silver from within, and when they open
their mouths, the teeth are translucent needles.

One notices him staring. She smiles.

Baby Boy looks away.

The singing gets louder.

---

They enter a cave system somewhere beneath the islands.
Baby Boy loses track of direction, of up and down. He
knows they're swimming through stone passages barely
wide enough for bodies, his tank scraping against rock, the
darkness total except for the faint bioluminescent glow of
the guardians' scales.

The singing follows him through the stone. Changes
pitch as the tunnels narrow and widen. Echoes off limestone
in ways that make it sound like more than one voice — like
a chorus just out of reach, harmonizing with something in
Baby Boy's chest.

Until — air.

They surface in a pocket of atmosphere that shouldn't
exist this deep in stone. Baby Boy rips off his mask and
gasps. The air tastes stale and mineral, but it's air, and he's
not drowning.

The guardians release him. He treads water,
looking around.

The cave is massive — easily a hundred feet across, the ceiling lost in shadow. And everywhere: light. Bioluminescent algae covers the walls in patterns that pulse gently, casting everything in blue-green glow. The water reflects it back, doubling the light, making the whole space feel alive. Breathing.

And the singing — here it's everywhere. Like the cave itself is humming.

And there are guardians. Hundreds of them.

They line the rocks at the water's edge, tails curled beneath them, watching. Baby Boy's heart hammers as he takes in the scope of what he's seeing. These are families, not just warriors. There are children — small and wide-eyed, their scales not yet fully formed, hiding behind their mothers. There are elders, ancient and scarred, their bodies marked with centuries of survival. There are mothers holding infants, rocking them gently, their webbed hands cradling tiny bodies that look more fish than human, more human than fish.

They're all staring at him.

Baby Boy's mouth goes dry.

One guardian gestures sharply, and the warriors who captured him haul Baby Boy out of the water onto a flat shelf of rock. He doesn't fight. They strip his gear — tank, vest, fins, everything. Leave him in just his wetsuit, shivering despite the humid warmth of the cave. His dive knife is gone. His collection bag with the stardust fragments. Everything.

Time moves wrong down here. He can't tell if hours pass or days. The bioluminescent light never changes — no sunrise, no sunset, only the same blue-green pulse. He sleeps and wakes and sleeps again and can't tell the difference. The singing fills the gaps.

*They brought me here for a reason. I need to figure out what.*

The guardians part, creating a corridor through their ranks. At the far end of the cave, something massive rises from the deep water.

---

She's enormous — easily fifteen feet from head to tail — and ancient in a way that makes his bones ache. Her scales are pale, almost translucent, like something that's been underwater so long it's lost its color. Her hair floats in strands of white and sea-foam green. High cheekbones. Sharp features. Eyes that glow pure silver.

She pulls herself onto the rock shelf with immense strength and deep weariness. When she settles, coiling her tail beneath her, Baby Boy realizes she's dying. The tremor in her hands, the labored breathing.

"Bring him closer," she says, and her voice is like stones in a current.

The warriors push Baby Boy forward until he's kneeling ten feet from her. Close enough to see the intricate patterns in her scales. Close enough to meet those silver eyes.

"You steal from us," she says.

Baby Boy's mind races. "We didn't know. We didn't know it was yours —"

"You thought the stars fell freely. That magic was yours for the taking." Her mouth curves. "Ignorance is not innocence, child."

Tala — the scarred one, the one who led the ambush — moves closer. "What shall we do with him, Mother Layka?"

The singing spikes. Sharp, like a finger pressed against a nerve. Baby Boy flinches and nobody notices. They're all watching Layka. But the sound is coming from Tala. From the fragment in Tala's chest. The one that glowed brightest in the water. The size of a fist, set into the high center of her sternum, pulsing blue-white.

It's singing to him.

He forces himself to focus. To listen to the words and not the sound.

The ancient guardian studies Baby Boy. "He looks like one of them. The two we took."

Baby Boy's heart stops. "What?"

"Ten years ago. Two fishermen stole from us. Jaime and Marcus. Do you know these names?"

Baby Boy can't breathe.

"I see you do." She leans closer. "Which one was yours?"

"Marcus." His voice cracks. "Marcus is my father."

"The one we couldn't break," she says.

"What?"

"Your father. Marcus." Layka's silver eyes hold steady. "The other one — Jaime — we bound the pearl to him. He became ours. Our captain. Owned. A weapon we drive through the deep. But Marcus." She tilts her head. "We tried the pearl on him first. It slid off him like water off oiled stone. He had something old in him our magic could not bind."

"What."

"The gold in his eyes when the light caught them right — the warmth of the sun. The same as yours, child. The sun-brother's line. The blood that resists ours." Her gaze drops to Baby Boy's face. "We could not own him. So we offered him service without the pearl — sworn, not bound. He refused. So we put him in iron and dropped him in the dark, where his refusal could not threaten us. And we let him watch what we made of the other."

"You're lying. My father drowned. Ten years ago. He's dead."

"Is he?" She gestures, and two warriors swim into a dark tunnel at the back of the cave. "Let me show you."

Baby Boy waits, every nerve strung tight.

The warriors return, dragging something between them. Someone.

Baby Boy sees the chains first — iron, rusted, wrapped around skeletal wrists and ankles. Then the body. Skin stretched over bones, corpse-pale from ten years without sunlight, covered in scars that never healed. Long hair, matted and gray, falling past shoulders that used to be broad.

They drop him on the rock shelf.

The man doesn't move. Just lies there breathing shallowly.

Baby Boy stares.

The face is wrong — gaunt, hollow, aged past recognition. But the eyes. When they open, just a crack.

Brown eyes. Warm brown.

His eyes.

"Dad?" The word comes out broken.

The man's head turns. His eyes focus with obvious effort.

"Baby Boy?" His voice is rusted, barely human. "My son?"

Baby Boy lunges forward. The warriors grab him but Layka makes a gesture and they release. He crashes to his knees beside his father, hands hovering, not knowing where to touch without causing pain.

"Dad. Oh god. Dad, you're alive —"

"So big." Marcus's hand reaches up, shaking violently, to touch Baby Boy's face. "You were just a baby. You were just —"

They're both crying. Marcus's tears stream down his hollow face, and Baby Boy holds his father's skeletal hand against his cheek and can't stop shaking.

The singing fades, pushed back by grief.

"I'm getting you out," Baby Boy says. "I'm getting you out of here."

Marcus makes a sound that could be a laugh or a sob. "Can't. The chains. Only Hook can break them."

"Hook?"

"The captain." Marcus's eyes close. "Jaime. Jack's father."

Marcus's eyes open again — urgent, ten years compressed into one desperate moment.

"That night on the boat. We were coming back from the crater — had the stardust in our bags. Thought we were safe." Each word costs him. "Tala came up from the water. Jaime didn't see her coming."

Baby Boy's grip tightens.

"She wanted the stardust back. Her razor teeth —" Marcus shudders. "She bit through Jaime's hand. Clean through the wrist. Blood everywhere."

He coughs, dry and rattling. His body isn't used to speaking this much.

"The other guardians came then. Dozens. Dragged us both underwater. Everything went black. The stardust kept us alive somehow — the fragments, the proximity. When I woke up we were here." His voice drops to almost nothing. "Jaime was screaming. They'd fused a hook to his wrist — metal and magic grown into his flesh. And they put something around his neck. A pearl. It — it changed him. Bound him. He stopped being Jaime."

Marcus's hand finds Baby Boy's arm.

"He's their captain now. The man I knew is gone." His eyes are wet. "I've watched him for ten years. He doesn't remember his own name most days. Just follows orders."

"Dad —"

"Listen to me." Marcus grabs Baby Boy's wrist. His eyes go wild. "The pearl controls everything. The ship in the fog. The dead it commands. Him. These chains on me. If you can destroy it — if you can break it —"

"How?"

"I don't know. I just know it's the source. Ten years I've watched it glow around his neck and every time she gives him an order the pearl pulses and he obeys. DESTROY THE PEARL. Promise me."

"I promise, Dad. I promise."

Marcus's hand falls. His eyes lose focus.

---

The warriors drag Marcus away.

Marcus's eyes burn into Baby Boy's, delirious.

"DESTROY THE PEARL!" His voice cracks, raw. "SON! IT'S THE SOURCE — IT'S THE SOURCE OF EVERYTHING!"

A guardian strikes. Marcus's head snaps back. Unconscious.

Baby Boy watches until he disappears into the dark tunnel. Then turns to face Layka.

The singing comes roaring back. Louder than before. As if Marcus's grief opened something in Baby Boy's chest that was holding it at bay, and now there's nothing between him and the sound.

"You tortured him for ten years. For what? Because he took some rocks?"

"Because he stole from us." Her voice is calm. Patient. "When you steal from us, you starve our young. You take the food from their mouths."

She gestures to the cave around her. The hundreds of guardians. The children hiding behind their mothers.

"I have watched this for five hundred years." Her eyes hold no anger, only exhaustion. "The Spanish came first. I sank their ship." She says it the way you'd say *I took out the trash*. "Five hundred years of protecting what should never have needed protecting."

"Then let us go. Let my father go. We won't come back."

"I cannot kill you, child." Layka's voice shifts — something almost like regret. "You carry the gold in your eyes — the warmth of the sun. The sun-brother's line. The same blood your father carries — faint, almost asleep, but there. Killing you would be killing family."

Baby Boy stares. "What?"

"It is the line that resists ours. The line the pearl cannot own. That is why I kept your father alive. That is why Tala brought you here instead of drowning you in the channel."

"I don't understand —"

"You don't need to. Not yet." Layka settles back. "But understand this: I cannot let you leave. You've taken from us. You'll take again. You'll bring others." Her voice is final. "So you stay. In chains, like your father. Where you can never hurt my children again."

The panic should be overwhelming. But the singing isn't letting him panic. It's rising through his chest like heat, pulling his attention toward —

Tala. Three feet to Layka's left. The scar in the center of her forehead, old and deep. And below her collarbones: the fragment. Pulsing blue-white. The source of the singing.

Baby Boy can feel it in his ribs now — past sound, into vibration. The stone calling to something in his body that he didn't know was there. The old blood Layka just named, answering a voice it's been deaf to for centuries.

*Don't.*

The thought is his own. Rational. Afraid.

*Don't reach for it. You don't know what it'll do.*

But his hands are tingling. His chest is pulling forward, physically, like a magnet in his sternum. The fragment is singing and his body is answering and the answer is: *yes, here, finally, home.*

*STOP. Think. You don't know what —*

"I understand," Baby Boy says. His voice is steady.

Layka nods. Begins to gesture to the guards.

# Chapter 17
# THE LONG SWIM

Baby Boy moves.

His body crosses the ten feet to Tala before his mind gives permission — legs pushing off stone, arms reaching, everything he has aimed at the light in her chest.

Tala's fast. Her hand comes up, claws extending, mouth opening to scream —

But Baby Boy has momentum and desperation and the weight of whatever is calling him, and his hand closes around the fragment in her chest.

And pulls.

The fragment doesn't want to come free.

It's embedded deep — fused to her sternum. But he pulls with everything the stardust gives him, and something in the fragment HELPS — reaches back, WANTS to come free.

It tears loose.

Flesh and blood come with it. Tala's scream is inhuman — the sound of something ancient torn out of her, something she's guarded so long it might as well have been her own.

The fragment burns in Baby Boy's hand. Actually burns, searing his palm, and he tries to drop it but can't. He CAN'T. It's pulling toward his chest with a force that has nothing to do with gravity. Like two magnets slamming together. Like something finding what it's been looking for.

The fragment hits his sternum and the world goes white. It strikes his chest like a fist and FUSES, burning through wetsuit, through skin, lodging against bone with a sound Baby Boy feels but doesn't hear.

Heat explodes through his body. Power floods through him the way light floods through glass. His vision goes white, then sharpens until he can see individual scales on faces across the cave.

The singing stops.

Silence.

Total, absolute silence, for the first time since they dragged him down.

He's never felt so strong.

He's never been so terrified.

Guardians swarm — dozens launching themselves at him. Baby Boy moves without thinking, the fragment making him fast. Faster than he's ever been.

A guardian from the left. He shoves her sideways — too hard, she crashes into the cave wall. Another from the right — he throws her back. They come and he fights through them, not trying to hurt, just moving, always moving, the fragment giving him strength that doesn't feel like his own.

A warrior with a spear drives it at his chest. He catches the shaft, snaps it, pushes her away.

Somewhere behind him, a child is screaming.

The sound cuts through the power like cold water. He's fighting in front of children. In their home.

Baby Boy's vision tunnels. He needs to get out. Behind Layka — a dark opening in the cave wall.

He runs. Pushes through guardians, shoving, deflecting, the fragment making him strong enough to move ancient beings aside. His wetsuit is torn. His chest burns where the fragment pulses in time with his heartbeat.

He reaches the tunnel and dives.

Narrow, barely wide enough for his shoulders, and lightless. Baby Boy swims blind, hands outstretched, his knuckles cracking against limestone on every stroke. Behind him: the sound of pursuit. Bodies cutting through water. Fast and closing.

He kicks harder.

The fragment radiates heat from his chest — a fist-sized sun burning through his sternum — and the contrast with the freezing water makes his whole body feel wrong. Hot center, cold everything else. Like fever and hypothermia happening at once.

His hand hits a wall. No. A turn. He twists left, scraping his shoulder raw against the stone. The rock is jagged here, porous, coral-crusted edges tearing through neoprene and into skin. He can feel the blood but can't see it.

The pursuit is closer. He can hear the click of claws on stone. The displacement of water behind him — big bodies, moving fast, coming through the dark with the ease of creatures who were born in it.

*Faster. Faster.*

The tunnel narrows. His tank scrapes the ceiling. But the tank is gone, stripped in the cave. Just his body, the wetsuit, and the fragment. He turns sideways to fit, ribs pressing against one wall, spine against the other. The stone squeezes. His lungs can barely expand.

He's underwater, no regulator, no tank, swimming blind, and he can't breathe.

*I'm going to die in here.*

The fragment pulses. Heat floods his chest. His lungs stop hurting. The need for air fades enough to keep swimming.

The tunnel widens. His elbows can move again. He kicks with everything the fragment gives him, and the walls change. Smoother. The current shifts from stagnant cave water to moving water. Ocean current.

Light ahead. Blue.

He kicks toward it, scraping through a gap barely wider than his hips, and the stone releases him into open ocean.

He kicks for the surface and the fragment shoves him through the water faster than any human should move — forty feet, twenty, ten, the pressure releasing so fast his ears scream. His body has no business surviving the ascent.

He breaks the surface and the first breath nearly kills him — his body has forgotten how to want it. His lungs seize, then release, then seize again. He floats on his back, coughing, gasping, staring up at —

Stars. Millions of stars. The Milky Way spanning the sky in a band of white so thick it looks solid.

He floats for a long time. His body doesn't want to move. Every muscle shaking, not from cold, from the fragment, the heat still radiating through his chest, the power humming through his bones like a tuning fork struck too hard.

He rolls over. Treads water. Tries to figure out where he is.

The islands are distant shadows on the horizon. Low and dark against dark sky. He could be miles from El Nido. Miles from shore. Miles from anything.

And he can feel them in the water below. The guardians. Present without pursuing — a weight in the deep, watching.

Baby Boy starts swimming.

---

He swims for hours under the stars.

The fragment keeps him moving: heat against the cold, strength against the exhaustion. But it costs something. The warmth begins in his chest and spreads outward, and his skin goes strange — tight, tingling, like sunburn without the sun.

His hands go numb first. Then his feet. Then his forearms — a wrong kind of numb, like the nerves are rewiring.

*It's fusing to me.*

*This is what happened to Jaime. Except this isn't a cord or a bracelet. This is embedded. This is as close as it gets.*

He can't think about that now. He swims toward the faint lights on the horizon.

His arms burn. His kicks weaken. The fragment keeps his lungs working and his heart beating but it can't stop his muscles from failing.

The lights get closer.

He counts strokes to stay sane. One hundred. Five hundred. At a thousand he stops counting.

The water is warm here. Shallower. His foot brushes sand and the relief is so sharp it buckles something in his chest that might be a sob if he had the energy.

Dawn breaks as Baby Boy drags himself onto a beach somewhere south of El Nido. A fishing village he doesn't recognize. White sand. Coconut palms. A beached banca with a painted hull peeling in the sun.

He collapses face-first. Sand in his mouth. Sand in the cuts from the tunnel. Sand pressing against the fragment in his chest — the cold of it leaching into the ground beneath him.

He lies there and breathes. The sky going pink above him. A rooster screaming somewhere.

He rolls onto his back. Looks down at himself.

The fragment shows clearly through the torn wetsuit — embedded in his sternum, glowing blue-white in the dawn light, the cracked neoprene flapping around it. And spreading from it: dark veins. Spider-webbing across his chest, up toward his collarbones, branching like the roots of a tree. They end at his neck. For now.

He touches the fragment. Cold. Pulsing. Steady as a heartbeat.

He drags the torn neoprene over what's left of his sternum to cover it. The cloth tears more. He covers it anyway, holding it down with one hand.

Baby Boy forces himself to stand. His legs shake. His vision blurs. But the fragment holds him upright — not with care, with purpose.

He needs to get home.

The walk takes two hours through jungle and coast roads and the outskirts of villages where people stare at the half-drowned boy stumbling past in a torn wetsuit, chest glowing faintly through the neoprene, dark lines crawling up his neck. An old woman crosses herself. A child points. A dog follows him for a quarter mile and then stops, whining, unwilling to come closer.

He can't stop. The fragment won't let him, and he's not sure anymore whether that's a gift or a sentence.

By the time he reaches the stilt houses he's on his hands and knees. The walkways are too high for his legs. He claws toward the dock — knees, palms, knees, palms — the fragment burning cold against his sternum. The dawn sun beats on his back. Somewhere a voice shouts. Feet on planks. Hands reaching.

He gets one more pull onto the warm wood.

*I have to find Jack.*

He doesn't make it to his feet.

Everything goes black.

# Chapter 18
# HOMECOMING

Jack doesn't sleep for three days.

They search every channel, every cove, every beach within ten miles. Nothing.

On the third morning he walks to the longest dock — the same place he sat after telling Baby Boy's family. Sits with his legs over the edge. Stares at the water.

His hand goes to his pocket. The fragment. He wraps his fingers around it the way he always does — searching for the warmth, for the pulse, for Baby Boy's heartbeat echoing through the stone.

It's faint. Fainter than yesterday. Fainter than the day before.

Jack holds the fragment against his palm and closes his eyes, and the warmth gives him something: the shape of Baby Boy's hand in the dark water, the squeeze that meant everything.

The fragment pulses once — faint, reaching — and Jack holds on.

His mother finds him there.

She's been different since Baby Boy disappeared. More present, more aware, like tragedy shocked her back into the world. She sits beside Jack without speaking, and for a long time they exist together.

"You haven't eaten," she says.

"Not hungry."

"Anak —"

"I can't, Mama." His voice breaks. "I can't eat and sleep and pretend everything's normal when he's out there —"

She pulls him close, and Jack finally cries. Sobs into his mother's shoulder like he's nine years old again, like he's not the one who's supposed to hold everything together.

"He's not dead," Joyce says firmly. "I can feel it."

"How?"

"A mother knows." She touches his face. "And you'll find him."

Jack goes home as the sun sets. His sisters are unusually quiet — even the wild ones move around him carefully, like he might shatter. Lucia makes dinner. Mariana and the littlest sit close to him on the porch, one on each side, their small hands in his.

"Kuya Baby Boy is okay, right?" Mariana asks in a small voice.

"I don't know, little fish."

"But you're going to find him?"

"Yes."

"Promise?"

Jack looks at his baby sister.

"Promise," he says.

He falls asleep on the porch sometime after midnight, too exhausted to make it upstairs, his sisters curled around him like they used to when they were small and scared.

It's full morning on the fourth day when he wakes — and there, crumpled at the far end of the dock where the planks meet the water, is a shape that wasn't there when he fell asleep.

At first Jack thinks he's dreaming. That figure, soaking wet, motionless — it can't be.

Then it moves. Drags itself up onto one elbow. And a voice, wrecked and barely there, carries across the morning:

"Jack?"

Jack is moving before his mind catches up. Off the porch, down the walkway, running full speed. Baby Boy is trying to push himself upright and failing, and he's there — actually there — folding back to the planks just as Jack reaches him.

"You're alive." Jack catches him before his head hits the wood. "You're alive. You're alive."

He's saying it over and over, hands running over Baby Boy's face, his shoulders, his arms — checking for injuries, for proof this is real.

Baby Boy is real. Solid. Here.

"Jack," Baby Boy says, voice hoarse. "I'm okay —"

"Don't you dare say you're okay." Jack pulls back to look at him properly.

Oh.

Baby Boy looks terrible. Wetsuit torn, skin covered in scrapes and bruises, hair matted with salt and blood, lips cracked. But that's not what makes Jack's stomach drop.

It's his chest.

Even through the torn wetsuit, the fragment is plain — embedded in his sternum, the dark veins cracking out from it like porcelain.

People are gathering on the dock now. An old fisherman sees the fragment and crosses himself. Behind him, a woman whispers a name Jack almost catches, old and reverent, that sounds like *Lisuga*.

"What is that?" Jack reaches out, stops before touching.

"The fragment from Tala's chest. I stole it." Baby Boy's voice is flat. "It's part of me now. I can't get it out." He looks down at the dark veins spreading across his chest. "I look like a road map."

"That's not funny."

"It's a little funny."

Jack stares at the fragment, at the veins. "We'll fix it," he says.

"Jack." Baby Boy's hand catches his. "There's something you need to know. About our fathers."

---

They move to Jack's porch — Baby Boy can't walk further, people are staring, this conversation needs privacy.

Lucia appears with water and food, takes one look at Baby Boy's chest, and goes pale. Her hand moves to her own sternum — involuntary, like the sight triggered a memory in her body. But she doesn't ask questions. Just leaves the supplies and ushers the younger sisters away.

Jack's mother stays. Sits in her chair, present in a way she hasn't been in years. Her eyes move between Jack and Baby

Boy — watching the way Jack's hands keep finding excuses to touch him. Adjusting the blanket. Brushing hair from his face. The constant, unconscious reaching.

She doesn't say anything. But her mouth softens, and she nods once — to herself, not to them.

Baby Boy drinks half the water in desperate gulps. Jack has to stop himself from reaching out every few seconds to confirm he's real.

"Tell me," Jack says. "Everything."

So Baby Boy does. The cave. The hundreds of guardians — families, children, elders. Being dragged before Layka, ancient and dying. The accusation: they stole from the sea. Their children are starving.

"They didn't know we didn't know," Baby Boy says. "To them we're just thieves."

"We are thieves," Jack says quietly.

"Yeah."

Then Baby Boy takes a breath. "They brought out my father."

Jack goes still.

"He's alive. Marcus is alive. He's been chained in their caves for ten years." Baby Boy's voice cracks. "I saw him. Talked to him. He's — he's a skeleton. Barely there. But alive."

"And yours," Baby Boy continues, quieter. "Your father is alive too."

Jack doesn't move. Doesn't blink. Just sits there as the air leaves the porch.

"Dad told me what happened that night." Baby Boy's voice is careful. Measured. "They were coming back from the crater. Tala came out of the water and attacked them. She — she bit through Jaime's hand. They dragged them both under."

Jack's jaw locks. His hand goes flat against the porch railing. Pressing hard enough that the grain digs into his palm.

"They put a hook where his hand was. Metal fused to flesh. And a pearl around his neck — Dad said it controls him. Changes him. He's their captain now." Baby Boy finally looks at Jack. "They call him Captain Hook."

The name lands and Jack stands up. Walks to the railing. Grips it with both hands.

He doesn't speak. Just stares at the bay — the water, the stilt houses, the limestone cliffs turning gold in the morning light. The same view he's had every day of his life. The same water his father disappeared into ten years ago.

Didn't disappear. Was taken. Was made into something.

His mother is crying silently behind him. He can hear it — the soft, suppressed sound she makes when she's trying not to be heard. The sound he grew up with.

"You knew," Jack says without turning.

"I suspected." Her voice is barely a whisper. "The violence in him, those last weeks. The drinking, the stardust, the way he looked at his own hands like they belonged to someone else. I knew he was capable of terrible things." She sobs once. "I just hoped the ocean would stop it."

Jack's knuckles are white on the railing. The wood creaks under his grip.

"Layka — the queen — she said my eyes carry the warmth of the sun," Baby Boy says. "The sun-brother's line. The blood that resists hers. That's why she couldn't kill me. Her magic can't touch the gold in me." He looks at Jack. "My father has it too. It's why she chained him instead of breaking him. The pearl wouldn't take him."

"And my father?"

Baby Boy is quiet for a moment. "Jaime didn't carry the gold." He looks at Jack, and his voice drops. "Neither do you. Whatever's in me that they couldn't own — you don't have it. So the pearl took him. They made him their captain. Put it around his neck. He stopped being Jaime." He pauses, and the next part costs him. "It could take you the same way."

Jack is still. His back to the porch. His face to the water.

"Dad said Jaime never aged. Ten years and he looks exactly the same. The pearl keeps him alive. Keeps him young. Keeps him theirs."

"Dad said to destroy the pearl," Baby Boy continues. "He said it's the source of everything: the ship, the crew, the binding. If we break it, we break what holds Hook."

"We can save Marcus too. The pearl controls the chains. Destroy the pearl, free him."

"So we face him," Jack says. His voice sounds like someone else's. "My father. What he became."

Baby Boy's hand finds Jack's arm. "Together."

Jack turns. Looks at Baby Boy — really looks. The fragment glowing in his chest. The dark veins spreading.

"You're corrupting," Jack says. "Like they did."

"I know." Baby Boy touches the fragment. "I can feel it. The cold. It's changing me and I can't stop it."

"We'll find a way."

"Jack —"

"We will." Jack grabs his hand. "I'm not losing you."

Baby Boy stares at him, and his face breaks open.

"I hear you," Baby Boy says quietly.

Arthur and Jodi arrive twenty minutes later, drawn by the commotion. Arthur takes one look at Baby Boy's chest and goes pale.

"Christ. Is that —"

"Tala's fragment. Kind of stuck."

"That's not stuck, love," Jodi says faintly. "That's embedded."

Arthur crouches down, studying it. "Does it hurt?"

"Constantly. Cold. Like ice in my chest." Baby Boy hesitates. "And the emotions are flattening. Everything feels distant."

Jack and Arthur exchange a look.

Baby Boy's jaw tightens. "I'm fighting it."

"I know you are," Arthur says gently.

The screen door opens. Lola Rosa is standing there — small, white-haired, eyes red from three days of weeping for a grandson she thought was dead. She's been at the house since Baby Boy's family arrived, sitting with Joyce, the two mothers holding each other's grief.

But now she's looking at the fragment in Baby Boy's chest with an expression Jack has never seen on her face. Recognition.

"You have to go see your grandmother," Lola Rosa says. Her voice is rough but steady. "Lola Carmen. South of here. You remember her, anak. She came after the fathers disappeared."

Ten years but Jack can still see her. The small woman with the dark eyes. The cigarette. The hand on his head, brief as a passing thought.

"She's still alive?"

"Still alive. Ten years on the islands now." Lola Rosa looks at Arthur. "She's babaylan. The real thing — stronger than I ever was. And if anyone can read what's in that boy's chest, it's her."

Arthur straightens. "Where exactly?"

"Half a day by boat. Maybe less. I can tell you how to find her."

"When do we go?" Baby Boy asks.

"Tomorrow. Rest first."

"We don't have time to rest —"

"Your Majesty," Jack says with a weak smile, bowing slightly toward Arthur. "With all due respect, we're not taking royal decrees on rest schedules."

Arthur's ears go pink. "I'm being practical —"

"You're being British," Jodi says, and Baby Boy laughs — thin and tired but real.

The sound makes Jack's chest ache with relief.

---

That afternoon, the porch is quiet. Sisters at school. Arthur and Jodi preparing for tomorrow. Joyce inside making food.

Jack reaches into his pocket. The fragment is still there — his half from the first dive. He wraps his hand around it and the warmth comes, but different now. Baby Boy is right here beside him, real and breathing, and the fragment gives back something simpler than the dark water: *he's alive, he's alive, he's alive.*

Baby Boy keeps touching the fragment — fingering the edges where it's fused to his skin.

"Stop," Jack says gently, catching Baby Boy's hand. "You'll make it worse."

"It can't get worse."

"It can. It will." Jack doesn't let go of his hand. "Tell me what it feels like."

Quiet. "Like drowning from the inside. Like ice spreading through me." He looks at Jack. "I'm scared."

"I know. Me too."

"Of me?"

"For you."

Baby Boy's eyes are wet.

"When I was down there," he says quietly. "In the dark. Fighting my way out. All I could think was: *I have to get back to him.*" He swallows hard. "You're the most important person in my world. You know that?"

"Yeah?"

"Since we were kids. I never said it. Never knew how. But down there I thought I might die and you'd never know —"

Jack leans forward and kisses him.

Soft. Careful. Baby Boy's lips are chapped and taste like salt water and three days of being gone.

For a moment Baby Boy doesn't move. Just holds still, like he's not sure this is real.

Then he makes a small sound, somewhere between a breath and a word, and kisses back.

Jack's hand finds the side of Baby Boy's face. His thumb traces the edge of the dark veins along his jaw, and he doesn't care. Baby Boy's hand comes up to Jack's wrist and holds it there, keeps Jack's palm against his cheek. Nothing matters except that Baby Boy is here and alive and kissing him back.

The porch. The evening air. The sound of the bay. Everything else falls away.

They break apart slowly, foreheads pressed together. Both breathing hard. Both crying a little.

"I thought you were dead," Jack whispers. "I thought I lost you and I never told you —"

"Tell me now."

"I love you. I've loved you since we were kids."

Baby Boy kisses him again, softer, and smiles against his lips.

"Good. Because I love you too."

They stay like that — foreheads together, breathing the same air.

"Since when?" Jack asks. His voice is wrecked.

"Since always." Baby Boy pulls back enough to look at him. "You?"

"I don't know when it began. I just know I couldn't stop."

"You hid it well."

"I hid it terribly. Lucia knew. The whole village probably knew."

"I knew." Baby Boy's grin is back — that reckless, wide-open grin, the one that makes Jack's chest fill up. "I was waiting for you to catch up."

"Ten years is a long time to wait."

"Twelve, actually. I was ahead of you by at least two years." He touches Jack's face — his cold fingers tracing Jack's jaw, his cheek, the line of his eyebrow. Memorizing. "You were worth it."

Jack makes a sound that might be a laugh or might be a sob, and kisses him again because he can, because Baby Boy is here and alive and grinning and saying the things Jack has wanted to hear for longer than he can count.

Just them.

---

That night, after everyone leaves, Baby Boy asks: "Can I stay here?"

"Always," Jack says.

They lie together on the porch, not quite sleeping, memorizing the sound of each other breathing.

"Tomorrow we see Lola Carmen," Jack says quietly. "She'll know how to fix this."

"What if she can't?"

"Then we find someone who can."

"And if there's no fix?"

Jack pulls him closer. "Then we find a new definition of okay. Together."

Baby Boy is quiet. "Jack?"

"Yeah?"

"I'm glad I came back to you."

Jack's throat tightens. "Me too."

They fall asleep tangled together, Baby Boy's head on Jack's chest, Jack's arms wrapped around him.

# Chapter 19
# EVERY MORNING

Morning.

Jack wakes first and doesn't move. Baby Boy's head is still on his chest, his breath slow and even. His face in sleep looks like the boy Jack has known his whole life.

Jack lies there and memorizes it.

The sunlight shifts through the porch slats, striping them both with gold. A rooster screams somewhere. A tricycle buzzes past on the road below. The sisters are still asleep upstairs — Jack can hear Mariana's soft snoring, the creak of someone rolling over.

Baby Boy stirs. Opens his eyes. The gold has dimmed — Lisuga eating it, taking the warmth back to herself. The brown going darker behind it. But still his.

"Morning," Baby Boy says.

"Morning."

"You're staring."

"Yeah."

"Do I have something on my face?"

"Dark veins and impending doom. Otherwise no."

Baby Boy laughs. The sound is thinner than it used to be, but it's real. Jack's whole chest fills with relief, for once.

"Pandesal?" Jack asks.

"Always pandesal."

Jack goes to the kitchen. Heats oil. Fries eggs — the last three from the neighbor's chickens. Burns the garlic slightly because he's rushing. Pulls pandesal from the basket and warms them on the stove the way his mother used to, pinching the rolls and sliding them over the heat.

He brings the plate out. The warm rolls in a folded cloth.

Baby Boy eats slowly, like he's reminding his body what food is for. Eggs too salty. Garlic burned. Rolls hot. He says "Best breakfast I've ever had" and Jack knows he's lying and doesn't care.

They sit on the porch afterward. Shoulders touching. Baby Boy's hand finds Jack's. His fingers lace with Jack's and hold.

"We should do this every morning," Baby Boy says.

"Burned eggs and bad garlic?"

"You. Me. The porch. The morning." He squeezes Jack's hand. "Just this."

Jack looks at the bay. At the water catching the early light. At the stilt houses waking up, laundry going out on lines, smoke rising from cooking fires.

"Just this," Jack says.

They sit there for twenty minutes. Maybe thirty. Baby Boy's head drifts to Jack's shoulder. Jack's thumb traces circles on his knuckles. Neither of them talks about the fragment or the cure or Lola Carmen or what comes next.

They exist in the same space, breathing the same air, holding hands on a porch in El Nido.

It's the best morning Jack can remember.

---

The next morning, Baby Boy drags Jack out of bed at dawn.

"Come on. Before anyone wakes up."

"Where?"

"Twin Peaks. The tree."

Jack stops pulling on his shorts. "You can barely walk."

"I can swim."

"You're sick, Baby Boy."

Baby Boy laughs — thin but real. "It's the only thing might make me feel better. Please."

Jack looks at him. At the dark veins, the pale face, the grin that hasn't quit. He pulls on his shirt.

They take the banca — the old one, the leaky one they've been paddling since they were kids. Baby Boy rows because he always rows, arms working the water with that easy strength that still startles Jack even though he's seen it a hundred times. The warmth pulses quiet between them. Steady.

Twin Peaks rises out of the morning haze. The two jagged rocks leaning together like old friends. The small crescent beach between them. The banyan tree.

They beach the banca and wade ashore. The sand is cool under Jack's feet. The tree is bigger than he remembers (ten years of growing, roots spreading wider, branches reaching further), but the shape is the same. The trunk they carved their initials into is still there, the letters swallowed by bark but the scars visible if you know where to look.

Baby Boy stands under the branches and looks up. Sunlight filters through the leaves and catches his face. The dark veins visible at his jaw, the pallor that wasn't there a week ago.

"Race you," Baby Boy says.

"To where?"

"Out and back. Like when we were kids."

"You always lost."

"I was eight. My arms were the size of breadsticks." He's already pulling his shirt off. "Now I have advantages."

They swim out past the shallows into the deep blue between the peaks. The water is clear enough to see the sandy bottom thirty feet below — sea grass waving, a starfish moving so slowly it looks painted on.

Then the turtle.

It rises from the sea grass like a dream — green shell the size of a table, flippers rowing lazily, ancient head turning to regard them with one dark eye. It hangs there for a moment, suspended in blue, and then turns and glides.

"Follow it," Baby Boy says, and dives.

Jack dives after him.

The turtle moves slowly enough to chase but fast enough to stay ahead — leading them down, deeper, past the sea grass into open water where the reef starts. Coral in colors Jack hasn't seen before: purple, orange, a blue so bright it hurts. Fish scattering around them. The turtle banking left around a coral head, and Baby Boy following, and Jack following Baby Boy, and all three of them moving through the water like they belong there.

Jack realizes he hasn't taken a breath in a long time. No chest-burn, no clench. He doesn't think about why.

He looks at Baby Boy. Baby Boy is ten feet ahead, chasing the turtle around a cluster of brain coral, and he isn't holding his breath at all. His cheeks aren't puffed. His body is relaxed. He's swimming. Breathing the water somehow. Baby Boy can feel the guardians' strength in his chest — old water, old line.

The turtle slows. Settles onto a ledge of coral and tucks its flippers in, done with them. Baby Boy hovers beside it, reaches out, and touches the shell with one finger. The turtle doesn't move. Just looks at him with that ancient, patient eye.

Baby Boy turns to Jack. Underwater, without masks, without regulators, with nothing between them but clear water — he reaches for Jack's hand.

Jack takes it.

They float there, twenty feet down, holding hands beside a sleeping turtle, and Jack thinks: *How long have we been under?* Three minutes? Five? His lungs are starting to ask. Baby Boy's aren't.

Baby Boy points up. They kick together. Jack rises hard, lungs burning by the time he breaks the surface. Baby Boy comes up beside him, breathing easy. The sun is higher now. The peaks cast shadows across the water.

"How long was that?" Jack asks, treading water.

"No idea. Long."

"Too long. Way too long."

"Are you complaining?"

"I'm stating a fact."

"Facts are boring." Baby Boy floats on his back, arms out, face to the sky. He is smiling. The real one. The one that's been lighting up Jack's world since they were eight.

"For a second down there," he says quietly, "I felt alive again. Like before."

Jack doesn't speak.

"But it pulls me, Jack. The fragment. Every time I'm in the water. It wants me to go back to the caves."

Jack's stomach tightens. "Then we don't go in the water."

"I know." Baby Boy is still floating. Eyes closed. "But it's not loud. It's patient."

Jack treads water beside him.

"Jack?"

"Yeah?"

"I'm happy."

The word lands strange. Simple.

"Me too," Jack says.

They swim back to the beach and lie in the sand under the banyan tree. Wet and breathing hard and close enough that Jack can feel the chill of him. Baby Boy's skin is colder than it should be but warmer than yesterday.

"We should do this every day," Baby Boy says.

"We have things to do."

"Yeah. But after."

"After what?"

"After everything. When it's fixed. When the fragment is out and I'm normal again and we don't have to steal from the ocean or fight ghosts or worry about anything." He turns his head. Looks at Jack with those gold-flecked eyes. "I want this. Every morning. The banca. The water. You."

Jack's throat tightens.

He reaches for Baby Boy's hand. Finds it. Holds it.

"Every morning," Jack says.

Baby Boy squeezes once. Then closes his eyes and lies there in the sun, and Jack watches the light move across his face.

But for now — for this one morning — it's enough.

# Chapter 20
# THE BABAYLAN

That evening, the sisters help pack.

Lucia presses bread and salt into Jack's hand. Mariana stuffs an extra blanket into the bag for Baby Boy. One of the little ones stands in the doorway, gravely watching.

Baby Boy sits at the kitchen table while Jack ties off the bag. The veins have crested his cheekbones since this morning.

A footstep on the stairs.

Joyce.

She moves like she's not sure her feet remember the floor. Lucia drops what she's holding. Jack stands very still.

Joyce doesn't look at her children. She walks across the kitchen to Baby Boy. Stops in front of him.

Then she puts both her hands on his chest, over the fragment.

She doesn't speak. She closes her eyes.

Baby Boy's breath catches. Not pain. The opposite. Warmth where there has only been cold. The dark veins along his jaw shimmer, recede a fingernail's width.

Then surge back, darker.

Joyce opens her eyes. Tired. So tired.

She reaches for Lucia's hands. Lifts them. Presses them to Baby Boy's chest, exactly where her own had been.

Lucia gasps — feels the warmth low in her palms, alive.

Joyce looks at her daughter. Speaks, her voice rusty from how little she uses it.

"Lola can teach you."

Then she walks slowly to the chair by the wall and sits. Mariana goes to her, and Joyce's hand finds her daughter's cheek and stays there.

Nobody moves.

"What was that?" Baby Boy whispers.

Lucia stares at her own hands. They are warm.

"I don't know," she says. "But I have to find out."

---

They leave at dawn: Jack, Baby Boy, Arthur, Jodi, and Lucia on the Endless Summer, motoring south along the coast. Lucia insisted on coming. Jack tried to argue. She gave him the look — the one that's been shutting down arguments since she was seven — and climbed aboard without another word. The morning is overcast, the water gray instead of its usual turquoise, the air heavy with moisture and the smell of coming rain.

Baby Boy sits at the bow wrapped in a blanket despite the humid warmth. He's been freezing since he returned — cold radiating from the fragment in his chest like it's pulling heat from the air around him. Jack sits beside him, close enough to feel the chill rolling off the fragment.

They're moving faster now. Yesterday they stopped at his collarbone. This morning they've reached his jaw.

"How do you feel?" Jack asks.

Baby Boy considers. "Distant. Like watching myself from far away." He touches the fragment through his shirt. "And angry. But it's not my anger. It's borrowed."

Baby Boy goes quiet for a long moment. Then: "I can barely feel you anymore. Through the warmth. Used to be so loud."

Arthur steers them through a narrow channel between two unnamed islands. Lucia stands at the bow reading off the slip of paper Lola Rosa drew up that morning — south past the mangrove line, through the gap between the two islands with no names, into the cove that smells like burning herbs.

"She helped me once," Jodi says. "Years ago. Parasite from bad water — local doctors couldn't figure it out. She fixed me in twenty minutes with herbs and prayer." She pauses. "But she's intense. Be respectful. Answer honestly. And don't touch anything in her cave."

"Why not?" Jack asks.

"Because some of it will kill you."

Lucia doesn't look up from her notebook. "She won't bite. She's my grandmother."

Jodi blinks. "She's your what?"

"My mother's mother. She used to live with us. Until I was four." Lucia closes the notebook. "She's been sending things ever since."

Jack glances at her. He'd known about the packages — books, dried plants, carefully wrapped jars arriving every few months without explanation — but not that Lucia had been keeping a path back ready in her head all this time.

---

They anchor in a small cove surrounded by mangroves. The water is murky brown, and the air smells like rotting vegetation and herbs burning, or incense, sharp enough to make Jack's sinuses tingle.

A narrow path leads inland through the mangrove forest. They pick their way over roots and rocks, sweating in thick humidity. The forest is alive with sound — insects, birds, things moving in undergrowth — but it all feels muffled.

After fifteen minutes, the path opens into a clearing.

The cave entrance is a dark mouth in the limestone cliff face, easily twenty feet tall. Vines hang across the opening like curtains. The stone around it is carved with symbols Jack doesn't recognize — spirals and circles and shapes that shift when he doesn't look directly at them.

Lucia steps to the cave mouth before anyone else can. "Lola." Her voice is barely loud enough to carry. "It's me."

Silence.

Movement in the darkness.

She emerges slowly. Smaller than Jack remembers, much smaller, the way old people get smaller, but the same dark eyes. Jack hadn't expected the memory to come back this clearly. The hand on the top of his head. The smell of dried herbs and wood smoke.

Lola Carmen is tiny, barely five feet, and thin to the point of translucence. Her skin is the color of mahogany, lined with wrinkles so deep they look carved by water over centuries. Her hair is pure white, hanging to her waist in a single thick braid. She wears a loose cotton dress and no shoes, and around her neck hang three things: a small cross, a strand of dried sampaguita, and a tooth — curved and yellowed and too large to be human.

But her eyes. Her eyes are dark, the brown so saturated it's almost black, like wood stained from decades of oil — the patina of a woman who has been handling stardust fragments for sixty years, not the void of corruption.

The neighbors call her babaylan. Healer.

Her gaze finds Lucia. Stops there.

For a moment nothing in her face moves. Her hand rises to her mouth.

"Anak," she says quietly.

"You said you'd come back for me." Lucia's voice doesn't shake but her hands are clenched at her sides. "I couldn't wait."

"I'm late."

"You said before the gift dies. It hasn't died."

"No. It hasn't." Lola Carmen takes one step forward. Touches Lucia's face. Her thumb traces the line under Lucia's eye like she's checking a stitch in old cloth. "I see you, anak."

Then her gaze moves to Jack. "Jack." He doesn't know what to say back.

She turns to Baby Boy.

"You children come to me after you've broken everything and expect me to fix it." Her voice is surprisingly strong. "Do I look like a mechanic?"

"We need help," Jack says.

"Obviously. What else would bring five people to an old woman's cave at dawn?" She steps closer to Baby Boy. "How long has that been in your chest?"

"Is 'too long' a medical term?" Baby Boy asks.

Lola Carmen almost smiles. "Sit, boy. Let me see what you've done to yourself."

Inside, the cave is larger than it should be, walls extending back into darkness. Candles burn everywhere, hundreds of them, casting shadows that dance. The air is thick with incense and loam, earth and growing things.

The walls are lined with shelves. Jars of dried plants and herbs, some labeled in Tagalog, some in a script Jack doesn't recognize. Bottles of coconut oil infused with flowers. Bundles of dried leaves tied with red thread. A mortar and pestle stained dark with decades of use. And on a high shelf, its own small altar: a Santo Niño beside two carved wooden figures — old, smooth, eyeless — and a bowl of white crystals that catch the candlelight.

Lola Carmen's altar. Like Joyce's, but complete.

Baby Boy sits cross-legged on a cleared space at the center of the stone floor. Jack sits beside him immediately.

Lola Carmen crouches in front of Baby Boy with surprising grace. Her fingers, twisted with arthritis, reach toward the fragment.

She doesn't touch it. Instead she takes a white crystal from the bowl on her altar (alum, Jack realizes, the same tawas crystals he's seen at market stalls) and holds it over a candle flame. The crystal melts slowly, dripping into a clay bowl of water she's placed between them.

The melted alum hits the water and hisses. Forms a shape.

Lola Carmen studies it. Her dark eyes narrow.

"Lisuga," she whispers. Not a question.

She reaches for the fragment now. The moment her skin makes contact, she hisses and jerks back.

"The fragment you tore from Tala's chest," she says. "The First Star." She laughs, a sound like wind through dry bamboo. "Oh, child. You're either the bravest fool I've ever met or the most foolish brave one."

"Both," Baby Boy says.

"Both." She leans closer, studying the dark veins spreading from the fragment. "It's fusing to you. Becoming part of your body. Lisuga's flesh binding to your bones." She sits back. "Days, and it reaches your heart. Then you'll be gone. What's left will look like you, move like you. But it won't be you."

"Can you remove it?" Jack asks.

Lola Carmen's black eyes fix on him. She studies his face a long time. Quieter: "Your mother's line. My line."

Lola Carmen touches the cross around her own neck. "Your mother's people were healers, anak. My people. Before the Church told us to forget. Women who could hear things others couldn't: the water speaking, the spirits moving through the world." She lets the cross drop. "But the gift needs tending. Needs teaching. And the ones who did the teaching were silenced three hundred years ago."

She stands slowly. "But first — before cures — you need to understand what's happening to him."

She picks up a small pot from her shelf. Heats oil over a candle, coconut oil, fragrant, mixed with herbs. As she talks, she rubs the oil into Baby Boy's chest around the fragment, chanting softly. The words shift between Latin (fragments of Catholic prayer) and something older, something that sounds like the language Lola Rosa whispers in.

"The sky father had three children." Lola Carmen's hands work the oil into Baby Boy's skin. He winces. She doesn't stop. "A daughter, Lisuga — silver, the stuff of his own heart. And two sons. The golden one, the bright restless one — he became the sun. The copper one, steady and quiet — he became the earth. The islands of Palawan are his hands."

Baby Boy stares at her. "I know the story. Lola Rosa told it to me when I was small."

"Then know it isn't a story." She presses harder. "The sons' blood walks the earth. The daughter's heart sank to the deepest water and her sea-children — the ones you call sirens — were born around it. They have always been of the sea. Silver in their eyes, like their mother. They have never been anything else."

She straightens. Looks at Baby Boy's face.

"You carry the sun-brother's light. The gold in your eyes is his mark. Faint, almost asleep, but his. Your father carries it too." Her dark gaze moves to Jack. "And you carry the copper-brother's line. Your mother's line. Mine."

She lifts her own face into the candlelight. Her eyes, that looked black in the gloom, catch the flame and shift — a thread of dull copper deep in the brown, like old wire under water. She tilts her chin so they can see.

"This is what we are. Children of the earth, of the brother of copper. We hear the water speaking. We hold the herbs that heal a child's sorrow. We tend the altar in the morning so the world stays right."

Her gaze flicks to Lucia, standing in the shadows.

"And she has it cleaner than I do."

Lucia's hand goes to her own sternum.

Lola Carmen turns back to Baby Boy. Touches the fragment in his chest.

"This is Lisuga's heart. The largest piece of her — the piece that held her soul. It has been in the dark for a thousand years, missing her brothers." Her voice softens. "When it found you — a boy with the sun in his blood — it reached for what it knew. The light it lost when the sky cracked. It is trying to come home through you. Pulling you back into what she was."

"So the dark veins —" Baby Boy says.

"Starlight eating gold. The goddess's heart taking the warmth back to herself." Lola Carmen sits back. "You are not being corrupted, child. You are being unmade. And the unmaking will kill you because you are too human to survive it and too kin to fight it."

The cave goes quiet.

Lucia, standing in the shadows near the entrance, hasn't moved. But her hand is pressed against her own sternum.

Lola Carmen's black eyes flick to her.

Lola Carmen turns back to Baby Boy.

"The healers knew how to approach Lisuga's fragments safely. Rice wine and betel nut and song. They would ask permission. The fragments would yield their power gently — as gift, not as invasion." Her voice hardens. "The Spanish burned the healers. Three hundred years of silence. And now nobody remembers how to ask, so they just take. And the goddess breaks them for it."

"Then how do I survive it?" Baby Boy asks.

Lola Carmen wipes her hands on a cloth. "There is a way. The pearl Layka made — you have heard of it. It is not a stone." Her voice flattens. "Five hundred years ago when the Spanish ships came, Layka called to the sky father for protection. She poured her blood into a clam at the bottom of the deep, and the father's grief — his tears, falling still from the night his children broke — answered. They mixed there. Salt and grief and a queen's blood. What grew was the pearl. It gave her power over the earth-children's blood. The colonists who came after were taken. Their ships sunk. The sea kept its own."

Her dark eyes move to Jack.

"Your father wears it now. He is the captain of the *Estrella Perdida* — the ship Layka took from the friar's bones five hundred years ago. The ghost ship in the fishermen's stories. She only sails at night, in heavy fog that moves against the wind. If you would find the pearl, you must find her. And to find her, you must find him."

The cave goes quiet.

"Hook," Jack says. His voice flat.

"Hook," she agrees.

She holds up a finger. "Right now, the pearl is the only thing keeping the boy alive. Its existence out there creates a balance. Siren magic holding goddess magic in check. Without it, Lisuga's heart would have finished him already." She lets the finger drop. "Bring it to me. Intact. I can use it to break the bond between the First Star and his body. The siren power overwhelms the fragment, loosens its grip. His body rejects it. He lives."

"And the pearl?" Arthur asks.

"The ritual consumes the pearl's power. When it's done, the pearl is empty. Dead glass." She pauses. "Which means everything connected to it collapses. The ghost ship. The drowned crew. The binding on Hook. All of it gone." Her voice is matter-of-fact. "Their weapon of protection, destroyed. They're defenseless against the next ship that comes." She looks at Baby Boy. "You live. They suffer."

Baby Boy is quiet.

"My father said to destroy it," Baby Boy says. "The pearl. Crush it. He said it's the source of everything."

"No." Lola Carmen's voice cuts. "Destruction and ritual are not the same thing. If someone crushes the pearl, just shatters it, everything collapses at once. No control. No direction. The shockwave hits every magical bond the pearl maintains, including the fragment in your chest." Her eyes are fierce. "Maybe the shockwave kills the fragment. Maybe it kills you. Maybe worse. Nobody knows. It has never been done."

She leans forward.

"Your father means well. But he has been chained in the dark for ten years, dreaming of a simple answer. Simple answers are dangerous." She grabs Baby Boy's arm. "Bring me the pearl intact. I will save your life. That I can promise. A shattered pearl is a gamble. And you do not gamble with the last of your time."

Silence.

Then Baby Boy, quietly: "Even the ritual — the pearl dying — that destroys the sirens' protection. I can't collapse a whole civilization to save myself. Their children —"

"Then you die in days," Lola Carmen says. "And become something worse than dead."

"There has to be another way," Jack says.

"There isn't."

"What if we cut it out?" Jodi asks. Her voice is tight — she's watching Baby Boy the way she watched her sister in the hospital bed in Coron, the same helpless recognition. "Surgery —"

"It's fusing to his heart. Cut it out, you cut out his heart. He dies on the table."

Jack's chest tightens. "So our options are: let him corrupt, or destroy an entire people's protection to save him."

"Yes."

"That's not a choice."

"It's life." Lola Carmen stands, joints creaking. "Choosing which loss you can survive." She moves to her shelves, pulls down a small clay jar. "This will slow the transformation. Not stop it. Buy you a few extra days." She hands the jar to Baby Boy. "Rub it on your chest twice daily.

Coconut oil, herbs, and my prayers sealed into the salve. It will hurt."

Baby Boy takes the jar with numb fingers.

She looks at Jack one more time. "You carry your mother's line, child. The copper-brother's blood, though it did not surface in your eyes. The gift skipped past you and landed in her." Her gaze moves to Lucia. "But you are still my grandson. Watch over her."

"Grandma." Jack's voice comes out cracked. The word doesn't fit his mouth and he says it anyway. "Thank you."

Lola Carmen's face moves — barely. Something close to a smile.

"Thank you," Arthur says. "For your honesty."

"Honesty is all I have left." She looks at Baby Boy. "Days. Maybe less."

She turns back toward the darkness of her cave. Stops. "You," she says.

The word is for Lucia, standing quiet by the entrance.

Lucia steps forward. Lola Carmen crosses the cave to her, moving differently now, no longer performing the fierce ancient but an old woman studying a young one's face with what looks like hunger. Or hope.

She takes Lucia's hands. Turns them over. Studies her palms.

"Mama did something," Lucia says. Her voice catches. "She came downstairs. Put her hands on Baby Boy. The veins moved." She opens her palms. "Then she put my hands where hers had been. It was warm."

Lola Carmen goes very still.

"She said you could teach me."

Lola Carmen closes her eyes. When she opens them they are wet. "My daughter," she says quietly. "After ten years of silence." She holds Lucia's hands tighter. "She still has it. It was only sleeping."

"When this is over," she says, "come back to me. Before the gift dies with me. Before there's no one left who remembers how it works."

Lucia nods. Once. Like a promise.

Lola Carmen releases her and disappears into the darkness of her cave.

The candles gutter.

---

They leave without speaking. Walk through the mangroves single file. Board the boat and find their places.

Arthur starts the engine. They motor away from the cove.

Baby Boy holds the clay jar, staring at it.

"Days," Baby Boy says.

Jack doesn't answer right away. His hands grip the railing. The water slides past — gray, flat, nothing like the turquoise of home.

"We'll find the pearl," Jack says finally. "We'll bring it to Lola Carmen intact. And we'll deal with the rest after you're alive."

"Jack —"

"After. You're alive."

Baby Boy looks at him. Those darkening eyes. "And if there's no after?"

Jack doesn't have an answer. He reaches into his pocket. The fragment is there — warm, pulsing, the echo of Baby Boy's heartbeat fainter every day.

He holds it and says nothing.

The boat motors north. Behind them, the mangroves close over Lola Carmen's cove like a curtain falling.

Jack watches the water.

# Chapter 21
# BECOMING STARS

The search eats them alive.

They sail by day and watch by night — every shipping lane between El Nido and Coron, every channel where a fisherman swears he saw three masts in fog that moved wrong, every cove a sailor whispered about and then crossed himself for whispering. Jodi radios every contact she has. Arthur cross-references his research with tide charts and moon phases and the patterns of every ship disappearance in the last fifty years.

Nothing. The *Estrella Perdida* surfaces when she chooses and no sooner.

Lola Carmen's instructions ride with them like ballast. *Find the ship. Find the pearl. Bring it to me intact.* Days, she'd said. The clay jar of salve she pressed into Baby Boy's hands buys a little time, not much. He works it into his chest twice a day, grits his teeth through the burn, and still the veins climb.

Jack stands at the bow watching the water pass, island after island, channel after channel, and reaches into his pocket. The fragment is there. His half. He wraps his hand around it and waits for the warmth.

It comes. But fainter than yesterday. The echo of Baby Boy's heartbeat, which used to pulse steady and sure against his palm, is getting harder to find. Like listening for a radio station that's drifting out of range. Still there. Just barely.

Behind him, at the stern, Baby Boy sits wrapped in a blanket despite the humid warmth. The dark veins have crept past his jaw and across his cheeks.

"You're staring again," Baby Boy says without looking up.

"Sorry."

"Don't be sorry. Just come sit with me instead of standing there looking tragic."

Jack sits. Their arms press together.

"How do you feel?" Jack asks.

Baby Boy considers. "Have you ever left food out too long and it goes room temperature? Not cold, not hot. Just nothing temperature?" He pulls the blanket tighter. "That. But everywhere. Inside."

"That's a weird metaphor."

"I'm losing my ability to make good ones. Next week I'll be comparing things to cardboard."

Jack almost smiles. But the joke has a flatness underneath it.

---

An old fisherman in Coron gives them their first lead — singing near the deep trench, three nights ago, the ocean itself crying. He marks a spot on Arthur's chart with a shaking hand and says: "You don't find it, boy. It finds you."

They search the coordinates for six hours. Find nothing. The water here is colder, darker. The kind of deep where sunlight gives up and turns around.

When they give up and turn the boat around, Baby Boy is standing at the railing — too still, his head tilted at an angle.

"Baby Boy?"

He turns. His eyes are nearly black now. Barely any gold left. Just dark.

"We should go," Baby Boy says. His voice is flat. "There's nothing here."

That night they anchor near a nameless island, just a crescent of white sand and coconut palms, the kind of place that doesn't have enough landmass to earn a name. Arthur cooks dinner on the Endless Summer's small stove. Rice and fish. The smell drifts across the deck (garlic and ginger and coconut oil) and Jack's stomach growls despite everything.

Baby Boy doesn't eat. Jack pushes a plate toward him. Baby Boy picks up the spoon. Puts it down. Picks it up again. Sets it on the plate. His hand moves in a loop: spoon to hand, hand to plate, spoon to hand.

"I don't feel hunger anymore," he says. "Or thirst. Or tired. Just nothing."

Jack reaches across and takes Baby Boy's hand. It's ice. The chill climbs Jack's wrist before he lets go.

"Can you feel this?" Jack asks.

Baby Boy looks down at their joined hands like he's studying a specimen. "I know I'm holding your hand. I can see it. I just can't feel it." A pause. The ghost of a smile flickers across his face. "Which is rude, honestly. I waited years for this."

Jack's throat seizes.

"I love you," Baby Boy says. "I know I do. I remember loving you. But it's like knowing a fact instead of feeling it."

Jack doesn't trust his voice. So he lifts Baby Boy's cold hand to his mouth and presses his lips against the knuckles. Holds them there. Breathes warmth into frozen skin.

Baby Boy watches him do it. His black eyes don't change. But his hand — just for a second — tightens.

Then releases.

"I'm sleeping on the bow tonight," Baby Boy says. "Alone."

"Why?"

"Because it's eating me, Jack. And I don't trust myself. I'm angry. All the time now. Like your father was."

"It's not me. It's what's left when the warmth goes." Baby Boy looks at his own hands. "I don't trust what I'll do while I'm asleep next to you. Let me keep you safe while I still want to."

"Okay," Jack whispers.

Baby Boy walks to the bow. Wraps himself in a blanket. Turns his back.

Arthur sits down beside Jack in the silence that follows. After a while: "The fisherman was right. We can't make her come — she'll come or she won't." He looks at the dark water. "But we can stop standing still. Tomorrow we hit a cargo ship. Move. Do something. Better than watching him fade."

Jack doesn't argue.

---

The Pacific Fortune appears on the horizon the next afternoon — a massive container ship heading south toward Manila, riding low and heavy with cargo. Registered in Singapore. Crew of twenty. No military escort.

The approach takes hours. They wait for dark. Motor close with lights off, engine barely audible. Jack sits on the gunwale, the hot metal of the outboard engine warming his legs through his shorts. The Pacific Fortune is lit up ahead: deck lights, cabin lights, navigation lights reflecting off the calm sea. A small city on the water, oblivious.

Nobody speaks. Even Baby Boy is quiet, sitting at the bow, head tilted toward the dark water.

The gap between the boats narrows. Two hundred yards. One hundred. Fifty.

Arthur and Jodi go up the hull first — ropes and grappling hooks, the familiar rhythm of the climb. Jack follows. Baby Boy is last, hauling himself over the railing with a strength that's too easy, too fluid.

The deck is wide and dark between the stacked containers. Somewhere forward, a radio is playing — tinny Filipino pop music, a woman singing about rain.

They move in pairs. Arthur and Jodi starboard. Jack and Baby Boy port.

A crewman appears around a container stack — young, holding a cigarette and a radio. His mouth opens.

Baby Boy is there before the sound comes out. He catches the man's wrist and twists. The bone gives way with a wet crack. The cigarette drops. The radio drops. The man makes a sound that isn't quite a scream — too high for that, almost a whistle.

Baby Boy's other hand goes to the man's throat.

"BABY BOY." Jack is moving but he's too far away.

The man's eyes are wide. His feet kick the deck. Baby Boy is studying his own hand on the man's neck like he's curious about the way it works.

"BABY BOY. STOP."

Jack reaches them. Grabs Baby Boy's shoulder. The muscle under his palm is iron.

For a long second nothing.

Then Baby Boy's hand opens. The man drops. Hits the deck choking but alive.

Baby Boy looks at Jack. The black eyes don't change. But his mouth makes the shape of a word he doesn't say.

They get the cargo and escape before anyone raises the alarm.

---

They climb back on the Endless Summer. Jack finds Baby Boy on the bow. The world is heavy between them.

"I would have killed him," Baby Boy says finally. "If you didn't stop me."

"I know."

"I'm so sorry, Jack. I'm so, so sorry."

"I can't make it stop." Baby Boy's voice cracks. "The anger doesn't stop. It's there when I close my eyes. When I look at you. When I look at my hands."

His shoulders break first. His chest second. He folds forward into Jack's arms sobbing — silent at first, then shaking, then sound coming out of him like something old and torn.

Jack pulls him tighter. The ice of him against Jack's collarbone. He cries until his shoulders stop shaking.

Jack holds his head. Strokes his hair. The dark veins under his thumb.

*I'll bring you back. Whatever it costs. I'll bring you back.*

"I've got you," Jack says into Baby Boy's hair. "I've got this. I'll take care of you."

---

Jack is lying on his back, staring at the stars, somewhere between sleep and thought — when Baby Boy's shadow falls across him.

"I can't remember your face anymore."

Jack sits up. Baby Boy is standing over him. His voice is flat.

"I know you're important," Baby Boy says. "I know I love you. But when I close my eyes I can't see you. Can't remember what you look like."

Jack's hand goes to his own mouth. Presses hard. Holds the sound in.

"I'm right here," he says through his fingers. "You don't need to remember. I'm right here."

Baby Boy sits beside him. Close but not touching. "Tell me something. About us. About before. So I know what I'm losing."

Jack tells him. The docks. The diving. The banyan tree. A lifetime of friendship that became something else without either of them naming it. The moment Jack knew. Baby Boy laughing while holding Mariana on his back, sunlight in his hair, looking at Jack over her head with that grin that made everything louder and brighter and more.

Baby Boy listens, his face giving nothing back.

"That sounds nice," he says when Jack finishes.

"It was."

"I wish I could remember it."

Quiet. The water laps. The Endless Summer rocks gently. Then Baby Boy, almost a whisper:

"I'm not going to be okay, Jack. Even if we get the pearl. I've hurt people. And I wanted to hurt them worse. That doesn't go away."

"We'll deal with —"

"If I don't make it. Move on."

"I don't want to survive this. I want you."

Baby Boy looks at him. Barely audible: "I want me too."

Jack reaches for his hand. Baby Boy lets him take it. For one moment — squeezes back.

Then lets go. Stands. Walks back to the bow.

Jack watches him go and the fragment in his pocket is colder than it's ever been. Almost nothing. The faintest echo, like a heartbeat heard through deep water.

---

They return to El Nido to resupply.

That evening, while Jack sleeps on the porch with his sisters curled around him, Lucia sits alone in the kitchen.

The altar is in front of her. The Santo Niño. The older carved figure. Fresh sampaguita she placed that morning, the flowers already wilting in the heat.

She lights a candle. Sits in the quiet.

The flame flickers. Steadies. Then flickers again. The air is still — the flame moves on its own, leaning toward the carved figure, as though drawn.

Lucia reaches out and touches the figure's smooth wooden head. It's warm. Not from the candle. From inside.

Her breath catches.

She closes her eyes and lets her palm press flat against the wood.

The warmth climbs through her hand into her wrist, then her chest. Slow. Steady. The way the figure has waited a thousand years to be touched like this.

And the figure shows her.

A ship — three masts, ragged sails, fog moving against the wind around the hull. Lucia knows she has never seen this ship and knows what it is.

A man on the deck. He has her brother's father's face but the eyes are wrong — blue-white where they should be

brown. His hand rests on a pearl at his throat. He is looking south. Looking for them.

*Three days,* a voice says. Not Lucia's. Not the figure's. Something older. *He comes for the star, child. Three days. Tell him. The boy with the gold can be saved.*

The vision lifts. Slowly. Like fog burning off.

Lucia opens her eyes. The kitchen is the kitchen again. The candle is still. The figure is warm under her hand. Her cheeks are wet.

She runs to the porch.

Jack is asleep with her sisters tangled around him. She kneels beside him. Touches his shoulder.

"Kuya."

He stirs.

"It's coming, kuya. The ship. Three days."

Jack's eyes open slowly. He doesn't ask how she knows.

# Chapter 22
# THE GHOST SHIP

Three nights later. Jack sits on his porch with Baby Boy, both staring at the bay, when it happens.

One moment the water is moving normally — gentle waves lapping at the stilts, the tide flowing in. The next: nothing.

Complete stillness.

"Jack." Baby Boy's voice is tight. "The water stopped."

The surface is glass. The cliffs and stars reflected with unnatural clarity. Every boat in the bay hangs suspended, motionless.

Then the fog comes.

It rolls in from the open sea — thick, moving against the wind. Glowing faintly green from within. It spreads across the water like oil, and everywhere it touches the air turns cold.

"Get inside," Jack says, standing. "Get my sisters —"

"JACK!" Arthur's voice from the Endless Summer anchored nearby. "FROM THE SEA!"

The village wakes. Doors opening. People emerging onto porches. Everyone can feel the wrongness in the air.

And through the fog:

A ship.

She materializes like a memory made solid — not sailing, not quite floating. There, suspended two hundred yards offshore. Massive. Ancient. Wrong.

The Estrella Perdida.

Three masts rise from her deck, broken and tilted, tattered sails catching wind that doesn't exist. Her hull is black with age and rot, wood that should have disintegrated centuries ago held together by magic and spite. Barnacles cover every surface. Algae glows along the waterline.

As Jack watches, rowboats lower from her sides. Three of them. And climbing down rope ladders —

Figures. Moving wrong. Too stiff. Too jerky. Heads turning at angles that living necks don't bend.

The drowned crew. Spanish sailors first — five hundred years of them, tricorne hats rotted to flaps, long brocade coats with tails hanging in shreds at their knees, brass buttons gone to verdigris. Then Filipino fishermen in salt-eaten cotton from every century since. A handful of modern tourists in faded board shorts. All dead, all enslaved. Skin gone gray-green, eyes glowing blue, bodies no longer fully human.

"Oh god," Jodi breathes. "There's so many."

The boats hit the water and the corpses row. In perfect unison. Sixty sets of oars moving as one, cutting through the still water without a sound.

Heading for shore.

"EVERYONE INSIDE!" Jack shouts. "NOW!"

The village erupts. Mothers grabbing children. Old men barricading doors. Father Miguel ringing the church bell — the alarm that hasn't been rung since the typhoon of 2013.

Jack turns to his house. His sisters are awake, crowding the doorway, eyes wide.

"Lucia. Take everyone upstairs. Board the windows."

"Jack —"

"Just do it." He looks at his mother standing behind Lucia. Joyce's eyes are clear. "Mama. Keep them safe."

Joyce nods once. Moves — actually moves with purpose — herding the girls inside. Already planning. Already protecting.

Baby Boy stands beside Jack at the railing, watching the boats approach. His black eyes reflect the fog's green glow.

"My father is on that ship," Baby Boy says.

"So is mine," Jack replies.

Arthur and Jodi climb onto the porch, both armed. "We should run," Jodi says. "Get everyone inland —"

"No time," Arthur says. "They're already too close."

The rowboats reach the shallows. The corpses step out in unison — dozens of bodies, boots splashing through water. They line up on the beach. Perfectly straight. Perfectly still.

Waiting.

Then one more figure climbs out of the lead boat.

Tall. Broad-shouldered. Moving with predatory grace. He wears the tattered remains of a Spanish captain's coat — dark brocade rotting to threads, hanging open over a scarred chest. Dark pants. Tall boots. Hair black streaked with silver, wild and long.

And his left arm —

Where his hand should be: a hook. Curved and wicked, the metal gleaming in the fog-light, fused to his flesh at the wrist. Magic and metal and skin grown together.

He walks forward, and the corpse crew parts for him.

Captain Hook.

Dad.

Even from fifty feet away, Jack recognizes that face. The bone structure he inherited. The jaw. The way he stands — weight on his back foot, ready to move.

But everything else is wrong. Skin corpse-pale, almost translucent. Eyes a cold blue-white, lit from within — no brown left in them at all, no warmth, just glow. His expression blank, like a mask of his father instead of the man.

And on his shoulder: a macaque. Small, Palawan-native, but wrong. Its fur matted and falling out, skin gray underneath, eyes glowing the same blue as the crew. Corrupted by the pearl the way the corpse crew is corrupted, but alive. Still breathing. The only living thing that chose to stay with him. When it sees Jack watching, it chatters. A sound like laughter through broken glass.

Hook scratches the macaque's head absently. The gesture is so familiar (Jack remembers his father doing the same thing to him, ruffling his hair after a good day fishing) that his throat seizes.

Then Hook speaks.

"So." His voice is deeper than Jack remembers. Colder. Completely empty. "My son."

"Don't call me that."

The pearl around Hook's neck pulses, a sharp blue-white flare. Hook flinches. His jaw locks. The macaque screeches. For a moment a tremor passes across Hook's face — someone pulling against a leash from the inside.

Then the pearl dims. Hook's face goes blank again.

Behind them, Arthur makes a small sound. Jack glances back. Arthur is staring at Hook, face gone white behind his glasses.

"You," Arthur says, stepping forward. "The bar fight. I pulled you off that tourist. That's how I got this ridiculous nickname."

Hook's empty eyes fix on Arthur. His jaw tightens — the only movement in that blank face.

"The British boy playing hero." Hook's voice drips with contempt. "'Gentlemen, please.' So polite. So noble." He spits the words. "They called you King after that. Long live the king. While I was the monster you saved everyone from."

"You were going to kill him," Arthur says.

"And you stopped me. Pulled me off. Made me look weak." Hook touches where his hand used to be. "You may have stopped me becoming a murderer that night, King. But the guardians came to finish what you started."

Arthur says nothing. The color has gone out of his face.

Hook's eyes study Jack's face. "You look like your mother. Same eyes." He tilts his head. "Is she still alive?"

"Yes. No thanks to you."

"Good." No expression changes. "Did she tell you how I used to hit her?"

Around them, Jack can feel the village watching —
his neighbors learning what his father was before he
became this.

"I was there," Jack says. "I remember."

"Then you know. I was already a monster." Hook takes
a step closer, boots silent on the sand. "The guardians just
gave me permission."

"You could have fought it. You could have chosen —"

"I chose survival. I'd do it again."

Baby Boy leans toward Jack. Barely a whisper: "He's
dramatic for a dead guy."

Then he steps forward. His black eyes meeting
Hook's empty ones.

"My father," Baby Boy says. "Marcus. Is he alive?"

Hook's gaze shifts to the fragment in Baby Boy's chest.
"You wear Tala's power. She wants you dead for that."

"Is my father still alive?"

"He's alive. In chains. Where I put him."

"Come to Snake Island. Tomorrow night. Midnight."
Hook touches the leather cord around his neck. The pearl
hangs from it — massive, perfectly round, glowing blue-
white. "Bring me the star in your chest. The one he tore
from Tala. I'll trade you the pearl for it. The boy lives. Village
stays standing."

"And if we refuse?"

Hook gestures to the corpse crew. "My masters prefer
their meat still screaming."

"Why trade the pearl at all?" Arthur asks. "It's
your power."

"It's my leash." Hook's lips curve, barely. "I want it off."

"Then throw it in the sea. Hand it to a stranger."

The pearl pulses. Hook's jaw locks — that tremor again, someone straining against the inside of his own face. When it passes, his voice is flat. "It does not let me give it away. It lets me do one thing: bring back what they sent me for." His blue-white gaze settles on the light in Baby Boy's chest. "They cannot walk on land. They want the heart returned — at any cost — so they made one of their own who could come ashore. I am the hand that reaches where they cannot." He touches the pearl. "But a trade, the magic permits. An exchange. So I offer you one. The only one I'm allowed."

"Why tell us where?" Baby Boy asks. "You could ambush us."

"Because I want you to know it's a trap. And you'll come anyway."

"Why would we walk into a trap?"

"Because you're desperate." Hook touches the pearl. "The fragment is killing you. Days left. You need this." He lets the pearl drop. "And you —" He looks at Jack. "You need to save everyone. Can't help yourself. You'll come to save him, save Marcus, save the village. Even knowing it's a trap."

He's right.

"See you tomorrow, son," Hook says.

Jack's jaw locks. He doesn't answer.

Hook half-turns. Then stops, like the thought just occurred to him.

"And — in good faith."

He raises one hand. On the deck behind him, the corpse crew parts. Two of them drag a body down the gangplank —

iron chains rattling against the rotted wood, bare feet barely touching the boards. They haul him to the surf, lift him over their heads, and throw him.

Marcus lands hard in the wet sand at the water's edge. The chains do not break. They strike rock and shudder and hold.

"Take him," Hook says. "He's useless to me. He never quite became one of mine."

Baby Boy is already moving. He hits the surf at a run and goes to his knees in the wet sand beside his father. Marcus's wrists are raw and scarred from ten years of chains, his hair matted gray.

But when Baby Boy touches his face, Marcus's eyes open.

"Anak?" Barely a whisper. "Baby Boy?"

"I'm here, Dad. I'm here."

Marcus's hand trembles as it finds Baby Boy's face. His fingers trace the dark veins, the black eyes, the fragment in his chest.

"What did they do to you?" Marcus whispers.

"You're free, Dad. That's all that matters."

On the ship, Hook watches. His face does not change. The macaque on his shoulder goes very still.

Then Hook turns and walks back across the deck. The corpse crew follows in formation. Within minutes the boats are rowing back through the fog.

The ship fades — not sailing away. Just fading. Translucent, then gone.

The fog lifts. The water moves again.

Nothing to prove what happened except footprints in the sand and an entire village that watched Jack's father reveal himself as a monster.

---

The village has come down to the water. Catalina pushes through the crowd, sees the body in the surf, and her knees nearly give. Lola Rosa holds her up.

"Marcus?" Catalina whispers. "Is that —?"

She wades into the wet sand. Drops to her knees beside her husband. Reaches for him and doesn't know where to touch. Her hands hover over his ruined body like she's afraid he'll shatter.

"Lina." Marcus's voice. Rusted.

Catalina makes a sound that isn't a word and pulls him close. He weighs nothing.

"I'm sorry," Marcus whispers into her hair. "I'm sorry I'm sorry I'm sorry —"

"Don't. You're home. You're home."

They hold each other in the surf, and the village watches, and nobody speaks.

Lola Rosa kneels beside her son in the sand. The chains rattle as she lifts his face in both her hands.

"My boy," she whispers.

Marcus opens his eyes at his mother's voice. "Mama?"

Lola Rosa sobs and reaches for him with shaking hands.

---

They carry Marcus up the dock. The chains drag across the wood. Nobody tries to pry them off — not yet, not in front of the whole village.

Jack walks behind, Baby Boy beside him.

Arthur waits at the end of the dock. Quiet. He says only: "Tomorrow night."

"Tomorrow night," Jack echoes.

# Chapter 23
# LAST LIGHT

Baby Boy wakes to his father screaming.

The sound rips through the house, raw and animal, and Baby Boy is at Marcus's side before his own eyes fully open. His hands find his father's shoulders.

"Dad. You're safe. You're home."

Marcus's eyes fly open, wild and unseeing. Still in the hold.

He sees Baby Boy's face. The present crashes back.

"Anak." His grip is weak but desperate. "You're real."

"I'm real."

Baby Boy holds his father and waits for the shaking to stop.

Catalina appears in the doorway. Her face does the thing it's been doing since he came home: the attempt at a smile that doesn't land. She moves forward slowly, like approaching a spooked animal, and sits on the bed.

"You're so thin," she whispers, her fingers finding the sharp jut of his collarbone.

Marcus's hand covers hers. Trembling. "I'm sorry. I'm so sorry —"

"Don't. Don't apologize for surviving."

Baby Boy watches his parents. His father weeping. His mother trying to hold him without breaking him. Lola Rosa entering with rice porridge, feeding Marcus with a spoon because his hands can't hold one.

---

In the late morning, Arthur comes with a hammer and a steel file.

"Let me try," he says.

They sit Marcus in the kitchen chair. Catalina holds her husband's wrists. Arthur kneels on the floor and goes after the iron — first the file, then the chisel, then the hammer against an anvil they drag in from the workshop.

Three hours. Sweat on Arthur's glasses. Sparks. Bruises on Catalina's hands from holding the chains steady.

The iron does not yield.

Arthur sits back on his heels. Looks at his tools. Looks at Marcus.

"It's not the iron," Arthur says. "It looks like iron, it weighs like iron, but —" He taps the file against a link. The tool slides off without leaving a mark. "Tools can't touch this. It's the pearl that holds them. It was always going to be the pearl."

Marcus stares at his own wrists. He has known it for ten years — the pearl holds them shut, and only the pearl will open them. But hearing someone else say it out loud is a different thing.

"I have to be on the boat tomorrow," he says. "Whatever happens out there. I'm not staying on shore."

Catalina closes her eyes. Doesn't argue.

---

By afternoon, the village comes. Baby Boy sits on the porch watching neighbors bring food, elders offer blessings. Marcus receives them with quiet grace, but Baby Boy sees what the visitors don't — the flinch when someone moves too fast, the eyes tracking every exit. His father is home. And still in chains.

That evening, when the visitors have gone and the house is quiet, Baby Boy sits in the doorway of the kitchen and watches his parents.

Marcus is at the table. Catalina has made him soup — the same recipe she made when Baby Boy was sick as a child. Chicken and ginger and rice. Marcus holds the spoon with both hands. They're shaking so badly the broth spills before it reaches his mouth. He tries again. Spills again. His jaw tightens. The frustration of a man whose body won't do what it used to do without thinking.

Catalina reaches across the table and takes the spoon from his hands. Steadying him, not taking over. She wraps her fingers around his and lifts the spoon together.

Marcus eats. Slowly. His wife's hands guiding his.

Neither of them speaks. The silence is full of ten years. Ten years of her sleeping alone and him sleeping in chains and both of them wondering if the other was alive. The silence of two people who have to learn each other again from scratch, because the man who left is not the man who came back, and the woman who waited is not the woman he left.

Catalina's free hand finds Marcus's cheek. He flinches, reflex not choice, and she pulls her hand back. Then puts it back, slower. He lets her.

"I'm sorry," Marcus whispers. "I'm sorry I'm sorry —"

"Stop apologizing for surviving," Catalina says — fierce and gentle at once. "You're here. You're eating. That's enough for today."

Baby Boy watches from the doorway. His father's hands in his mother's steady ones. The soup. The silence.

He turns away before they can see him watching.

---

Inside Jack's house across the bay, they're gathering stardust. Every fragment from the dive, wrapped in cloth, laid out on the kitchen table. Baby Boy should be there helping, but his legs feel heavy and the porch rail is the only thing keeping him vertical.

He touches the fragment through his shirt. The First Star, fused to his sternum, edges visible through the fabric like a bruise made of light. The warmth should be there. Jack's warmth. The dive. The dark water. But it gives back nothing.

The goodbye happens in the kitchen.

Catalina makes tea. Baby Boy sits at the small table. And then he's crying, tears sliding down his face, silent and steady. He touches them, confused.

"I don't know why I'm crying," he says. "I can't feel it but it's happening anyway."

Catalina takes his hands.

She presses her lips together hard enough to go white.

"Do you love him? Jack?"

And Baby Boy breaks. Whatever ice the fragment has built around his insides, this question cracks it.

"Yes, Mama. Yes. Always. Since we were kids. It's always been him." His voice cracks. "But it's distant now. It's being taken from me. It's turning cold."

She holds him despite the cold radiating from his chest.

"You're so cold," she whispers. "Like you're already gone."

"I'm still here. I promise." He doesn't sound convincing. "Mama. I'm going to be fine."

She looks at him. Those eyes that have always been able to read him.

"Okay. I'm not going to be fine. But I'm going to be brave, which is almost the same thing."

"Mama, I'm so scared." The words surprise him. He didn't know he was scared until he said it. "I'm scared of forgetting. Of becoming nothing."

"You won't forget. Love leaves marks."

"And if I'm not cured?"

"Then at least you fought for something. Your father refused them and they chained him for it. You're choosing to risk everything."

Baby Boy holds his mother and tries to remember what warmth feels like.

---

From the porch, Baby Boy watches Jack say goodbye to his family.

He can't hear the words through the window, only the tone. Joyce's voice, low and firm. Jack's voice, cracking. The sisters quiet for once. Mariana's small voice asking something that makes Jack go still.

Baby Boy watches Jack hold his mother. Jack's face over Joyce's shoulder — eyes closed, jaw tight.

*He's so afraid. He's always been so afraid.*

*And I've been waiting for him to not be. But maybe the brave thing was just showing up anyway.*

On the boat, Baby Boy takes the bow.

He doesn't choose it. His body goes there, the way it always goes to the tip of things. The edge of docks, the point of boats, the highest branch. He's always been the one who sits where the world drops away.

Behind him, his father sleeps in the stern, chains still on his wrists. Arthur steers. Jodi sits near the cabin. Lucia in the stern, near Marcus.

And Jack.

Jack is beside him. Always beside him. The boy who keeps his love hidden in his pocket while Baby Boy's burns visible through his chest for the whole world to see.

"Jack."

"Yeah?"

"I need to tell you this. In case it doesn't work." Baby Boy turns. His eyes are empty — he can see Jack flinch and try to hide it. "I know I love you. I remember it. I just can't get to it."

"I know."

"If I don't make it — don't blame yourself."

"I can't promise that."

"I know." Baby Boy's mouth does something — not quite a smile. "But I had to ask."

They sit. The water slides past. The sun is doing its beautiful thing with the sky, gold turning to pink turning to violet, and Baby Boy can see it but can't feel it.

Then, from deep inside the nothing, one last spark:

"Jack?"

"Yeah?"

"If this works and I survive, I'm going to eat so much pandesal. Like, an obscene amount."

Jack almost laughs. "And if it doesn't work?"

"Then I'll haunt the bakery."

Jack laughs. The sound of it reaches Baby Boy the way light reaches the bottom of the ocean. Dimmed. Refracted. Barely there. But there. He made Jack laugh. Even now. Even with his humanity burning away and his body turning to starlight and his heart going cold inside a goddess's fist.

He made Jack laugh.

That has to count for something.

---

Snake Island appears as the last light fades.

The small rocky outcrop with its single dead tree. The crater beneath it, dropping into deep water. The place where they first dove together. Where their hands found each other in the dark. Where everything began.

Arthur cuts the engine. They drift.

Marcus wakes. Looks around. Goes pale. "Ten years. I haven't seen this place in ten years."

Baby Boy takes his father's hand. Marcus's hand is warm. Baby Boy's is ice.

"It's going to be okay, Dad."

"I'm sorry." Marcus's voice breaks. "I should have never come here. Never stolen from them."

"You were trying to survive." Baby Boy's voice is flat but gentle. "We all make impossible choices. This is mine."

The stars come out. The water reflects them — doubled, infinite.

Baby Boy sits at the bow and looks at the sky. Somewhere up there, Lisuga's body is still scattered. Still pulsing.

He touches the fragment in his chest. The First Star. The goddess's heart, fused to a land-child.

*I'm becoming a star.*

The thought doesn't scare him anymore. Nothing does.

But beneath the nothing, deep and almost gone, a flicker. A warmth older than the fragment. There before the stardust, there after.

Jack's hand in the dark water. The squeeze that meant everything.

*Hold on to that. That's the last real thing you have.*
Baby Boy holds on.
The water is still. The stars are bright.

# Chapter 24
# THE TRADE

Midnight.

The fog comes first — thick and heavy and moving against the wind, rolling across the water like something alive. The ship. The Estrella Perdida materializing from nothing, suspended two hundred yards away, her rotted hull dripping darkness.

Hook stands at the bow. The pearl glows around his neck.

Jack and Baby Boy stand at the bow of the Endless Summer. Behind them: Arthur, Jodi, Lucia, Marcus — who insisted on coming, who can barely stand, who is here anyway.

Hook walks across the water toward them. Steps onto their boat like gravity is optional.

"The star," Hook says. His blue-white eyes settle on Baby Boy's chest. "Step forward, boy. I'll take it out clean."

Baby Boy starts to move. Jack catches his arm.

"The pearl first," Jack says.

"You don't trust me?"

"No."

Hook's head tips a fraction. "Smart." He reaches up, lifts the leather cord over his head. The pearl hangs from it — massive, perfectly round, glowing with five centuries of cold, swallowed light.

He holds it out.

Jack reaches for it.

Their fingers are about to meet —

---

Marcus has been watching. Waiting.

*Destroy the pearl. It's the source of everything.*

Ten years he's thought about this.

"NO!" Marcus's hand shoots out, grabbing the pearl from Hook's grasp before either Jack or Hook can react.

"Dad, stop!" Baby Boy gasps.

Marcus's fist closes around the pearl. His eyes burn with ten years of clarity.

"Anak. This will save you."

And he crushes it.

---

The pearl shatters. Five hundred years of it, let loose in a heartbeat.

Light explodes outward — blue-white brilliance that burns through closed eyelids. The boat pitches. Water leaps the rail. The air itself rips.

Jack is thrown backward, crashes into the hull. The boat slams sideways, water coming over the gunwale.

Through the blinding light he sees:

The Estrella Perdida wrenching upward. The corpse crew collapsing — all sixty of them dropping together, blue eyes fading to nothing.

Marcus's chains snap open at the wrists and ankles. Iron crashes to the deck. For the first time in ten years, his hands are his own.

Hook staggers, falls to one knee. The leather cord around his neck — empty now. He gasps, clutches his chest where the binding used to be.

"Free," Hook whispers. "Finally —"

But Hook is bleeding. Blood runs from his nose. His hands shake. The hook on his left arm flickers, the magic that fused it to his flesh wavering.

"The pearl kept you immortal," Arthur says, the words slow as he gets there. "Now you're —"

"Mortal." Hook touches his face, feels the blood. Mortal. Bleeding. His own blood on his own face. He turns his hands over, watches it run down to the wrist. "I can die."

Baby Boy screams.

---

Jack spins. Baby Boy has collapsed, hands clutching his chest. The fragment's light is wrong now — pulsing wrong, too bright, shot through with red.

"What's happening?" Jack drops beside him.

"The fragment —" Baby Boy gasps. "The pearl balanced it. Kept it stable. Now —"

His back bows off the boards as the fragment flares. The dark veins spread fast — visibly moving, up his neck, across his face, reaching for his eyes.

"NO!" Jack grabs Baby Boy's shoulders. "You're going to be fine —"

"Can't — fix —" Baby Boy's back arches. "It's — burning —"

Marcus crawls over. "Anak, I'm sorry, I thought —"

"You destroyed the only cure," Jack says, voice raw. "You killed your own son."

"I was trying to free everyone!" Marcus's voice breaks.

Baby Boy is barely conscious. Convulsing. The fragment so bright now they can't look at it. His skin going translucent, veins visible, bones showing through.

Dying.

The water breaks open. Guardians surface all around them — dozens, swimming fast, desperate, enraged. Tala leads them, the scar in her forehead dark against pale skin, her lips peeled back off her teeth.

"THE FIRST STAR!" The sound that comes out of her isn't a human sound. She stares at the fragment in Baby Boy's chest. "You stole the FIRST STAR!"

She lunges for the boat.

Hook moves. Still weak, still bleeding, but faster than human. His hand closes around Tala's throat mid-lunge.

"You enslaved me for ten years."

Tala claws at his hand. "We gave you a choice —"

"You gave me CHAINS."

Hook drives the hook up through Tala's throat. Dark blood pours over his wrist. She floats a moment. Sinks.

Gone.

The other guardians break over the rail and come at him. Hook fights — but mortal now. Easy to cut. Claws rake his back. Teeth sink into his arm. He throws them off, but more are coming. Too many.

He's bleeding. Weakening.

Jack watches his father fight for his life.

Baby Boy stops screaming.

The silence is worse.

Jack looks down. Baby Boy's eyes have rolled back. Breathing shallow, irregular. The fragment stuttering, too bright, then almost gone.

"Stay with me," Jack begs. "Please."

Baby Boy's eyes flutter open. The black is receding. Gold flickers. For the first time in days, Baby Boy looks like himself.

"Jack." Barely a whisper. "I can see you now. I can remember your face."

Heat floods Jack's eyes and spills over. "Good. Keep looking. Stay with me."

"Your eyes." Baby Boy's hand, trembling, weak, but his hand, his human hand, rises to touch Jack's face. His fingers are ice against Jack's skin. "I forgot how warm they are. Dark, warm brown. The way they look at me like I matter."

"You do matter. You're everything."

"I'm sorry." His voice cracks. Clear tears leak from his eyes. "For getting cold. For forgetting what you look like. For making you carry this alone."

"You didn't —"

"I did." Baby Boy's eyes hold Jack's. He's all the way here. "You've been carrying me. Carrying everyone. Since we were nine years old. Since you stood between your parents and chose to protect instead of being protected." His voice drops to nothing. "Who carries you, Jack?"

Jack can't answer.

"Promise me something," Baby Boy whispers.

"Anything."

"Don't become him." His eyes flick toward Hook. "Don't let me dying turn you into what killed me. Promise."

"I can't —"

"Promise." His grip on Jack's face tightens with the last of his strength. "Mourn me. Miss me. Be angry." His eyes cut to Hook. "But don't go where he went. Don't let it turn you into that."

"You are —"

"I'm not." His thumb drags across Jack's cheekbone, the smallest pressure. "Nobody is." And then the smile — the real one, the one Jack's been chasing since they were kids.

"Don't say goodbye. We promised — paradise, remember? Under the tree —"

"Not goodbye." Baby Boy's voice is fading. "Meet me in paradise. Promise?"

"I promise. I promise."

Baby Boy's hand slides behind Jack's neck.

Pulls him down.

Their lips meet.

Soft. Gentle. Baby Boy, all of him, here for this one. Human. His own. Just a boy kissing another boy he's loved since they were children playing on docks and carving names into trees and promising forever.

Jack tastes salt. Tastes blood. Tastes ocean and stardust and eighteen years of friendship and a few days of something more.

Every sunrise they'll never see. Every island they'll never explore. Every whispered *I love you* that will never be said.

All of it in this one kiss.

Baby Boy's hand slides from Jack's neck.

His lips go still.

They break apart slowly — so slowly — and Baby Boy's eyes meet Jack's one last time.

Brown.

Gold.

Warm.

Human.

His.

"You're so beautiful," Baby Boy whispers. Barely breath. "I'm glad it was you. That I got to — that you were the last thing I —"

He doesn't finish.

His eyes close.

The gold dims.

The brown fades.

The warmth leaves his skin.

The fragment stops glowing.

And Jack is holding a body that weighs too much and too little at the same time.

Baby Boy is gone.

Jack holds Baby Boy's body and just sits in the bottom of the boat, rocking slowly, whispering:

"See you in paradise."

"See you in paradise."

Over and over. If he keeps saying it, Baby Boy will hear. This isn't goodbye. Just see you later. Just wait for me. Just —

"Baby Boy?" The word comes apart. "Baby Boy, please —"

He presses his hand to Baby Boy's chest. No heartbeat. No breath.

Hook stands on the water nearby. Covered in guardian blood. Breathing hard.

And Baby Boy is cold in Jack's arms.

The grief hits his ribcage like a fist and keeps pushing.

His hand moves to the fragment embedded in Baby Boy's chest. Closes around it. The warmth floods through him. Power. Raw and total.

He knows what this will do. If he takes this into himself, the boy who promised to be different will be gone.

He looks at Baby Boy's face. The stillness.

He rips.

"Jack, DON'T —" Arthur's voice, distant.

The fragment tears free with a wet sound, and power, raw, absolute, floods through Jack from the contact point. Lisuga's flesh searing against his palm, tearing up his arm, into his chest. His eyes go black. His skin goes cold.

What's left flies.

---

Jack rises off the boat — gravity just letting go — and the dead boy's heart pulls him up into the night.

Up past the ghost ship's masts.

Up past the clouds.

Up until the stars are close and the moon hangs huge and silver behind him.

And for a moment he just hangs there. A boy, arms spread, black against the white of the moon. A boy who can fly.

But this isn't Neverland. This is vengeance.

A boy flying out to kill his father, a dead boy's heart going cold in his fist.

Then he drops across the sky like a falling star thrown in reverse — so fast the moonlight breaks around him, stardust tearing off his body in a long blue-white wake. And all of him is burning now. The grief has gone to rage, and the rage to one white-hot want: to reach the thing wearing his father's face and end it.

Arthur grabs the railing. "Oh my god."

But Jack doesn't hear.

The macaque screeches warning.

Hook looks up.

And Jack — full of Lisuga's flesh and his own black rage — slams into his father.

They hang suspended over black water, and Jack puts his face an inch from his father's:

"I WILL KILL YOU!"

Hook doesn't flinch. "Good. Then you'll become me."

"I DON'T CARE!"

Jack drives the fragment forward — still wet with Baby Boy's blood — and stabs it into Hook's chest.

Right where the pearl used to hang.

Right where his heart should be.

Light tears out of the wound, blue-white, turning night to day. The water boils. The air catches fire.

And Hook's head goes back, every cord in his neck standing out.

The fragment screams — not fusing, being forced. It fights him, pulling away. But Jack's rage drives it past skin, past muscle, and it lodges between Hook's ribs. Black corruption lines spread from the wound, the same thing that killed Baby Boy eating into Hook's flesh.

Up his neck. Across his face.

Hook and Jack fall. Hit the water hard. Jack tries to hold on —

The sea opens under them.

Layka surges from the depths.

Her body is still dying — but her children are dying faster, down in the dark without the heart that made them, and a mother will spend the last of herself to stop that. She comes up out of the black water vast and terrible. Scales rainbow-dark in the moonlight. Eyes the hard silver of mercury. Five hundred years in her face, every one of them bent on the star in Hook's chest.

She rises fifteen feet above the water. Her voice shakes the air:

"THE FIRST STAR!"

Her hands close around Hook's corrupted body. She rips him from Jack with inhuman strength.

"You're MINE now." She pulls him close. "Mortal. Wounded. Corrupted. Finally vulnerable."

She drags him down.

"I'll take you to the dark. To the trenches where light doesn't reach. Where a millennium is a moment." Her claws tighten. "I'll feed off the First Star's power. Forever."

Hook's eyes — corrupted, fading — drop to the fragment in his chest. His hand moves. Grabs it — the fragment that's been trying to tear free, that's been fighting the wrong blood since Jack drove it in.

And pushes.

The fragment fights him. Writhes against his palm. But Hook is raw will and ten years of choosing survival, and he forces it past the cage of ribs, past bone, into the hollow where his heart had been.

"NO —" Layka lunges. "DON'T —"

The First Star detonates.

The light that comes off his chest isn't blue-white anymore. Prismatic. Every color. The light of creation.

Lisuga's flesh, the body of a goddess shattered millennia ago, scattered across the stars, falling as meteors, gathered as stardust, concentrated in a single fragment, fuses with the space where Hook's human heart used to beat.

The black corruption lines don't stop the light. They channel it.

Hook throws his head back, the sound torn out of him. The sea hisses and steams. The ghost ship shudders, rises higher.

Layka releases him. She draws back through the water — Layka, who has not been afraid of anything in five hundred years.

"What have you done?" she whispers. "You've made it your HEART."

Hook floats in the water.

When he opens his eyes, they're not black anymore.

They're prismatic. The colors of stars being born.

"I chose survival," Hook says, and his voice rolls out deep enough to shake the water. "Again."

The light from his chest pulses steady. Rhythmic.

A heartbeat.

Lisuga's flesh has replaced his heart. A goddess's body beating in a colonizer's descendant's chest.

"You can't control that power," Layka says, backing away. "It will destroy you —"

"I already lost myself. Ten years ago."

He rises from the water. Standing on the surface. The ghost ship descends to meet him.

"You were going to enslave me," Hook says. "Feed off my suffering for a millennium."

"Yes." Layka's voice is small.

"Thank you. For teaching me that some choices are worse than death."

The ghost ship settles beside him. The macaque returns to his shoulder.

Hook boards his ship. It rises with him.

"The First Star is MINE!" Layka's cry chases the ship across the water. "It was hers since the sky cracked!"

"Then come take it," Hook says, touching his chest. "If you can."

He looks at Jack, floating in the water, holding Baby Boy's body.

"I'm sorry," Hook says, and for one moment his voice is Jaime's. "For everything."

The prismatic light flares brighter.

"But survival costs everything," Hook finishes. "You'll learn that when you hunt me."

The ghost ship rises higher, black against the stars. Gone.

---

Jack floats in the water. Layka surfaces beside him.

Not to attack — she stares at where Hook disappeared.

"What did he do?" Jack asks.

"He made himself unkillable." Her voice is unsteady. "The First Star isn't just power. It's creation. As long as it beats in his chest, he cannot die."

"Then how —"

"You can't." She looks at him. "Don't you understand? You did this. Your rage. Your grief. You gave him Lisuga's heart."

Jack stares.

"Your father was mortal. We could have killed him. But you ripped the First Star from your lover's body and gave Hook the one thing that makes him immortal."

"I was trying to kill him," Jack whispers.

"And instead you made him a god."

She sinks into the depths.

And Jack is left floating there, holding Baby Boy's body.

The water is warm. The stars are bright. The bay is still now. It doesn't care what just happened. It doesn't stop being beautiful because a boy died in it.

Jack holds him. He's heavy the way only the dead are heavy. Jack's fingers have gone white and his jaw is clenched so tight his teeth ache.

"I'm sorry," he whispers. "I couldn't save you. I couldn't stop him. I made everything worse."

Baby Boy doesn't answer.

Jack presses his face against Baby Boy's hair. Salt and blood and the cold mineral smell of the fragment that isn't glowing anymore. He breathes it in. Holds it. As if breath could bring someone back. As if sorry could reach wherever Baby Boy has gone.

Somewhere, Arthur is calling his name. Somewhere, Jodi is pressing both hands over her mouth. Somewhere, Marcus is making a sound into the water — raw, shredded, the sound of a father who survived ten years of chains only to watch his son die in front of him.

Jack doesn't hear any of it.

He holds Baby Boy in the warm water under bright stars and whispers the only words left:

"I'm sorry. I'm sorry. I'm sorry."

The water laps gentle against them both.

And somewhere in the sky, Hook flies free.

# Chapter 25
# BROKEN

They bring Baby Boy's body back to El Nido at dawn.

The Endless Summer motors into the bay as the sun comes up over the water. A perfect morning. The kind Baby Boy used to love.

The village is waiting. They line the docks and walkways, silent and watching. Everyone knows. Word spread through the night.

Baby Boy's mother sees them approaching. She's standing at the end of the main dock, Lola Rosa holding her upright, and the moment she sees the body wrapped in white cloth on the deck —

She screams.

Not a word. Just sound — the cry a mother makes when her child is taken.

"BABY BOY!" She collapses, and Lola Rosa catches her, both of them sinking to the dock. "MY BABY! MY BABY BOY!"

The village women swarm — holding her, weeping with her, keening in harmony. The mourning cry that's been sung in these islands for a thousand years.

Marcus climbs out of the boat first. Barely standing. His wife sees him — her husband alive after ten years — and the boat carrying her son's body.

She makes a sound. Just breaking.

Marcus stands alone on the dock. Free after ten years, but more alone than he ever was in chains.

Jack watches from the boat. Baby Boy's mother screaming. Marcus bleeding. The village witnessing their grief.

And he feels nothing.

They walk through the village in procession. Baby Boy at the front, wrapped in white cloth, carried by six men — Jack, Marcus, Arthur, Father Miguel, and two fishermen who lost family to the sea. Behind them: Catalina and Lola Rosa, supported by the women. Behind them: the whole village.

Past the stilt houses. Past the market. Past the church. Past everything familiar and unchanged.

They reach the banyan tree on the far side of the bay. The same tree where Jack and Baby Boy played as children. Climbed its branches. Hid in its roots. Carved their initials into bark that's long since grown over.

The tree has been here longer than the village. Will be here long after everyone is gone.

It feels right that Baby Boy should rest beneath it.

The village men dig the grave. Six feet deep. Lined with banana leaves. Father Miguel speaks prayers in Tagalog and Latin. The whole village attends — women in terno, men in barong, children in white. They bring sampaguita and white roses and hibiscus until the grave is covered in petals and the air is thick with their perfume.

Jack stands apart. His mother tries to reach him. He steps away.

Lucia stands near the tree, one hand pressed against the bark, the other against her sternum, the gesture she's been making since she first saw the fragment in Baby Boy's chest. But it's deliberate now, not involuntary. Like she's pressing the weight in to keep it from escaping.

She looks at Jack across the grave. Her face is wet but her eyes are steady. She doesn't try to speak. She knows the wall.

Jack doesn't respond to anyone.

They fill in the grave. The first shovelful of earth hits the cloth-wrapped body — a soft, heavy thud, like the world closing a door. His knees buckle. Arthur catches his arm. Jack stays standing, but only because Arthur won't let go.

Shovel by shovel, earth covers Baby Boy until he disappears.

The funeral ends as the sun reaches its peak. People begin to leave — slowly, reluctantly, touching Baby Boy's mother as they pass, murmuring condolences that won't help, offering food and prayers and presence.

Jack doesn't leave.

Stands there while the crowd disperses. While his family goes home. While Lola Rosa leads Marcus away, still bleeding. While the sun climbs higher.

Baby Boy is in the ground. Jack is still here.

He kneels at the grave. Touches the fresh dirt. The flowers.

"I broke my promise," he whispers. "You asked me not to become him. And I became him anyway. Worse than him. I gave Hook power. I couldn't save you."

The grave doesn't answer.

"I don't know how to live in a world without you. I don't know how to be me when you're the one who knew who I was."

The sun beats down. The banyan leaves rustle. The bay sparkles blue.

Then —

The ground warms under his palms.

Jack presses harder — not imagining it. It spreads through the earth beneath his hands. He sees it: the dirt around the grave beginning to glow. Faintly at first, then brighter. Gold light seeping up through the soil.

The gold spreads. Pools around the grave. Flows up the cliff faces, down through the beach toward the bay in glowing rivulets. And where it touches the water —

The entire bay ignites. Gold, not blue. Every reef, every cliff face, every inch of water catching the glow.

The village emerges. Points. Stares.

"It's Baby Boy," someone whispers. "He's saying goodbye."

The light pulses — once, twice, three times. Like a heartbeat.

And Jack's chest floods with it — the same warmth as the dive, as Baby Boy's hand in the dark water. Like Baby Boy is close, impossibly close, just for this moment.

He knows Baby Boy is here. In the light. In the water.

It fades, the gold dimming back to morning.

The warmth in Jack's chest fades with it.

*He died with nothing,* Jack thinks. *Couldn't save him. Couldn't stop any of it.*

"I'm going to kill him," Jack whispers to the grave. "You asked me not to. Your dad asked me not to. But I'm going to anyway. I'm going to learn how to kill a god."

The grave is silent.

Jack stands. Turns away. Walks down the shoreline.

---

Days after the funeral, Jack still wakes reaching. His hand finds the side of the mattress where Baby Boy should be. It is cold. He keeps reaching anyway.

His sisters know not to ask. Joyce knows not to ask. He stops eating. Sleeps in his clothes. Spends most days at the dock watching the bay where Baby Boy used to come from.

---

Two weeks after the funeral, Catalina finds Jack.

He's in his house, packing. Weapons. Supplies. Maps of the Sulu Sea.

"Where are you going?" Catalina asks from the doorway.

Jack doesn't look up. "Away."

"To hunt your father."

"Yes."

Catalina enters slowly. Sits on the floor cushion where Jack and Baby Boy used to sleep during sleepovers. She watches him pack with methodical precision.

Then: "I've known for years. About how he loved you."

Jack's hands still on the knife he's wrapping.

"Since you were children. I'd watch him watch you. The way his whole face would light up when you walked into a room. The way he'd find excuses to touch your shoulder, your arm, like he needed to make sure you were real." Her voice is soft. Aching. "I knew before he knew. Before he had words for it."

Jack's throat tightens.

"But he never said it out loud." Catalina's hand presses flat to her own chest. "All those years of loving you and being too scared to admit it."

"When did he —" Jack can't finish.

"After he came back. After the fragment was already in his chest." She wipes her eyes. "He came to me crying — confused because he couldn't feel why the tears were coming. And he finally said it. 'Jack. I love Jack. I've loved him since we were kids. It's always been him.'"

Jack's breath catches.

"He told me it was being taken from him. Turning cold. That he knew he loved you but couldn't feel it anymore. Like it was locked behind ice." Catalina is crying now. "My son finally found the courage to say he loved you, and it was only because he was losing the ability to feel it."

Jack can't breathe.

"I told him love leaves marks. That even when you can't feel it, it's still there." Her voice breaks completely. "I was lying. I knew he might not make it. But I wanted him to have hope."

Catalina reaches into her pocket. "He made this for you. After your father left. You were nine years old, holding your whole family together, and Baby Boy —" She can barely get it out. "He wanted you to know someone was holding you too."

She holds out a bracelet woven from threads, faded with age. And tied into the weave — small, pulsing faintly gold — Baby Boy's fragment. His half from the first dive. The one he'd kept in his pocket since the day he took the cord off.

"I found the fragment in his clothes before the burial," Catalina says. "Still in his pocket. Still warm." Her voice breaks. "He carried it every day. Even after the First Star was in his chest — he kept this one close. His piece of you." She touches the bracelet, the one Baby Boy wove at eight. "I tied the fragment into the threads here, where his fingers used to work. So he could give you both things at once. The love he carried and the love he made."

Jack takes it with shaking hands. The bracelet is simple. Childish. Made with clumsy fingers and patient love. He can see Baby Boy at eight, sitting on a porch, weaving threads while stealing glances at Jack in the water.

The fragment had always glowed the cold blue-white of the deep — Lisuga's light, the light that took their fathers. It doesn't now. It pulses gold. Warm gold, sun gold, the gold his eyes used to catch when the light hit them right. Like the last of him went into the last thing he made.

And it pulses against his fingers, warm, alive, carrying the echo of every time Baby Boy reached for it and felt Jack's hand in the dark.

Ten years ago. Before the raids. Before the stardust. Before everything.

When Baby Boy was just a boy who loved his best friend and didn't have words for it yet.

"He never gave it to you because he was too shy," Catalina says. "Kept it all these years. Waiting to be brave enough."

Jack ties it around his wrist, and the breath leaves him in a sound he doesn't recognize as his own.

"He loved you his whole life," Catalina whispers. "And I got to watch him love you. That's the gift he gave me."

She stands. Touches Jack's face.

"I don't know where you're going. I don't know if you'll come back. But I'm grateful. That my son got to love you. That you loved him back. That he died knowing what it felt like."

She kisses his forehead.

"Thank you," she whispers. "For making his life beautiful. At the end."

She leaves.

And Jack sits alone, holding the bracelet, feeling the last piece of Baby Boy against his skin —

And finally breaks.

Doesn't scream. Just weeps.

For the boy who loved him ten years in silence. For the life they could have had.

He cries until there's nothing left.

Then wipes his face. Ties the bracelet tight around his wrist. Feels the fragment pulse against his skin — Baby Boy's warmth, Baby Boy's hand, one last time.

He stands. Looks at the room. At the bag half-packed with weapons and maps.

He could stop. Stay. Grieve like a normal person, surrounded by sisters who love him.

But the fragment pulses again and the warmth shifts. Not Baby Boy anymore. A colder pulse underneath. The echo of the First Star. The moment on the boat when he held a goddess's heart in his fist and flew.

Jack picks up the knife — his father's knife — and slides it into the bag.

Before dawn, he goes to the kitchen. The house is dark. His sisters asleep in a pile, Mariana's arm thrown across one of the little ones. His mother in her chair by the window, sleeping upright.

The altar is where it's always been. Santo Niño beside the carved wooden woman. Lucia's fresh sampaguita wilting in the heat.

Jack reaches into his pocket. Takes out his fragment — his half from the first dive, the one he's carried for months, the one that used to pulse with Baby Boy's heartbeat and now pulses with nothing. Dead warmth. An echo of an echo.

He sets it on the altar shelf. Between the saint and the babaylan. Where Lucia will find it.

He tears a scrap from one of Arthur's notebooks still stuffed in his bag. Writes five words in bad handwriting:

*Don't hold it near your heart.*

He folds the paper and sets it beneath the fragment. Lucia will find both in the morning. She'll understand the gift. She'll understand the warning. She's always understood things before anyone explained them.

The fragment sits on the shelf, dim and quiet. The carved woman watches over it with her certain face.

He touches the bracelet on his left wrist — Baby Boy's half. That one goes with him.

He loads the banca at dawn. Weapons wrapped in cloth. Maps marked with ghost ship sightings.

Arthur and Jodi find him preparing to cast off.

"Let us come," Arthur says.

"No."

"You can't do this alone —"

"I have to."

Arthur cleans his glasses slowly. "Where will you go?"

"Manila first. The fight pits. I need to learn how to fight things that don't die." Jack unties the mooring line. "Then wherever the rumors lead."

"And when you find him?"

"I kill him."

"Even if it makes you exactly like him?"

Jack looks at them. "I don't have room to care anymore. All I have left is this."

He touches the bracelet.

"Come back," Arthur says, voice thick. "When it's done. Whatever you've become."

Jodi steps forward. Puts her hand on Jack's arm. Doesn't say anything for a moment. Then: "He would have hated this. You know that."

Jack knows.

He doesn't promise.

He pushes off from the dock.

"KUYA!"

Mariana's voice. Small and high and desperate. She's running down the walkway in bare feet, her school uniform half-buttoned, hair wild. The other sisters are behind her but Mariana is fastest — she's always been fastest when it matters.

She reaches the end of the dock just as the banca drifts beyond arm's length. Her hand stretches out. Her fingers close on air.

"You said you'd never leave," she says.

Jack's hands go still on the paddle. The water widens between them — three feet, four, five.

He doesn't have an answer. He had answers for everything — for the rice running low, for the permission slips, for the monsters in the water and the monster who was his father. He's had answers for ten years.

He doesn't have one for a ten-year-old girl in bare feet asking why her brother is breaking his promise.

"I'll come back," he says.

Mariana's face is wet. "You don't know that."

"No. I don't."

She stands there. The water keeps widening. Behind her, his mother appears on the shore. Lucia and the other sisters beside her. And beyond them — on porches, in doorways, at the edges of the walkway — the village. Watching. The same people who lined the docks when Baby Boy's body came home. Nobody calls out. Nobody waves. An old woman crosses herself. A fisherman takes off his hat.

She's humming. The wordless song. The one she sings when someone is being taken.

Lucia stands beside her mother, one hand resting on Joyce's arm.

But not now. Now she watches her brother row away. And when the banca is small enough to lose, she turns from the dock and walks home. Not to her room. To the altar. She kneels in front of the carved figure — the smooth-faced woman her mother used to pray to — and picks up the fragment Jack left there. Holds it in her palm. Cool now, almost nothing — an echo of an echo.

She doesn't put it near her heart. She read the note.

She puts it in the healer's book, between the pages where the recipes are, where the knowledge lives. Where it will be safe until she's ready.

The humming stops. "Don't take my boy," Joyce whispers into the wind.

Jack doesn't look back.

# EPILOGUE

*Three months later.*

The Coron fight pit smells like blood and old sweat and desperation.

It sits twenty feet underground, carved into limestone caves that tourists never see. You reach it through a fish market, down stairs slick with something that might be water or might be worse, past a door with no sign that everyone knows better than knock on unless you're looking for violence.

Inside: darkness broken only by oil lamps casting shadows that dance like ghosts. A ring of packed dirt stained rust-brown from years of bleeding. Spectators crowd the edges — fishermen betting their week's wages, merchants looking for entertainment, sailors from a dozen countries all speaking languages that blur together into white noise punctuated by screaming.

Tonight the crowd is loud. Bloodthirsty. There's a new fighter — young, vicious, undefeated in twelve fights across three cities. They're calling him a demon. A ghost. A boy with nothing left to lose.

They're calling him Warboy.

He stands in the center of the ring waiting for his opponent, and if you didn't know to look, you might miss him. He's unremarkable at first glance — twenty, maybe younger, average height, too thin like he hasn't been eating enough. Dark hair grown wild and long, falling into eyes that don't reflect the lamplight the way living eyes should.

But then you see how he stands. Weight perfectly balanced. Hands loose at his sides but ready to become fists in a heartbeat. Every muscle coiled like a spring waiting to release. He doesn't look at the crowd. Doesn't acknowledge the noise. Just stares at the opposite entrance where his opponent will emerge.

Waiting.

Patient as death.

The promoter — a woman with gold teeth and scarred knuckles named Rodha — climbs into the ring. "LADIES AND GENTLEMEN!" Her voice cuts through the chaos. "Tonight's final fight! Luis the Mountain versus the undefeated newcomer — WARBOY!"

The crowd roars.

Luis enters from the far tunnel. He's massive. Six foot five, two hundred fifty pounds of muscle and scar tissue. Arms like tree trunks. Fists that have broken bones and ended careers. He's won twelve fights tonight. The crowd loves him. Bets heavily on him.

He sees Warboy and grins, showing missing teeth. "You're a boy. A baby. I'm going to break you."

Warboy doesn't respond. Just watches Luis approach with those dead eyes, calculating exactly how this ends.

Rodha steps between them. "Rules are simple. Fight until someone can't. No weapons. No killing unless it's an accident." She looks at both fighters. "Ready?"

Luis cracks his knuckles. "Ready to make some money."

Warboy says nothing. But the corner of his mouth twitches — not quite a smile. Just a flicker of recognition, cold and patient.

Rodha backs away. Raises her hand. "FIGHT!"

Luis charges immediately, the way he always does. Pure aggression, assuming size and strength will win because they usually do.

Warboy waits.

Waits until Luis is three steps away, arm cocked back for a haymaker that could drop a horse.

Warboy moves — into the punch, not away from it.

Then Rodha sees it: the scar on his right palm blazing bright, a burn mark in the shape of something he once held, and the bracelet on his left wrist pulsing in answer — gold, steady as a heartbeat — and that gold leaps to his eyes and his feet leave the ground. Leave the ground. He flies. She gasps.

What —

But he's already landed, closing the distance, getting inside Luis's reach before the punch can land. His fist drives into Luis's kidney — once, twice, three times in rapid succession so fast it sounds like a drumroll.

Luis grunts, staggers. His punch goes wide.

Warboy's already moving. Circling. His leg sweeps Luis's knee — not to knock him down, to break it. The sound of cartilage tearing makes the crowd gasp. Some people turn away.

Luis screams. Goes down hard. Reaches for his ruined knee.

Warboy drops on him. Elbow to the temple. Precise, calculated, exactly enough force to disorient without killing. Luis's hands come up to defend. Warboy breaks his fingers. Methodically. One by one. The sounds are small and terrible — wet snaps that carry across the pit because the crowd has gone so quiet you can hear the oil lamps hiss.

"Stop," Luis gasps. "I yield. I —"

Another elbow. Temple again. Luis's eyes roll back.

The silence holds. Nobody breathes. The crowd that was screaming for blood thirty seconds ago can't look away and can't cheer. A woman near the back puts her hand over her mouth. A man who bet his week's wages on Luis doesn't move to collect.

Warboy stands slowly. Looks down at Luis's unconscious body. No satisfaction. No guilt. Nothing.

Just the mechanical completion of a task.

Rodha climbs back into the ring, staring at Warboy like she's seeing him for the first time. "Winner: Warboy."

Scattered applause. Nervous. No one's quite sure what they just witnessed.

Warboy holds out his hand. "A thousand pesos."

Rodha pays him with trembling fingers.

Warboy doesn't respond.

"You looking for work?" Rodha tries. "I could use a fighter like you. Make you rich."

"No. I'm looking for information." Warboy's voice is flat. "The Estrella Perdida. The captain who walks on water. Anyone seen her?"

The crowd murmurs. Everyone's heard the stories. The ship that appears and disappears. Bodies washing up on beaches with their throats torn out. Captain Hook's reign of terror.

"Last sighting was near Coron," someone calls from the back. "Three days ago. Fishing boat saw it rising from the water near the sunken ships of Olympia Maru."

Warboy nods once. Turns to leave.

Rodha watches the boy's back turn into the dark. The lamplight falls across him, and his outline casts not even a hint of a shadow on the stone.

"Wait," Rodha calls. "What's your real name? People want to know who you are."

Warboy stops in the tunnel entrance. Doesn't turn around.

"That is my real name," he says.

And then he's gone.

In the tunnel, alone, he stops. Leans against the stone wall. The adrenaline draining. His hands shaking — from what comes after, when the violence stops and there's nothing left to hit and the silence rushes in.

He touches the bracelet on his left wrist. The fragment woven into the threads pulses faintly, warm, steady — the rhythm he's known since the dive. Since the dark water. Since their hands found each other sixty feet down.

Maybe his own pulse. Maybe not. He doesn't ask.

Jack closes his eyes and holds it. Just for a moment.

Then he opens his eyes and walks into the dark.

---

El Nido.

The grave rests quiet under stars.

The flowers are fresh — changed this morning by Baby Boy's mother, who still comes every day. Who still weeps. Who still whispers to the earth as if her son can hear.

The banyan tree stands silent. The same tree where two boys played. Where they grew up together. Where they carved their initials and promised forever.

The wind moves through the leaves — soft at first, then stronger, carrying something that sounds almost like a voice.

*Mama?*

Catalina stops mid-prayer. Looks up at the rustling branches.

*Will he be okay?*

The voice is so faint she thinks she imagined it. Baby Boy's voice. Young and afraid.

She touches the fresh earth, tears streaming.

"I don't know, anak," she whispers. "I don't know."

The wind dies.

The tree goes still.

And in the bark, barely visible in the moonlight, she sees the carving. Fresh. Raw. Cut deep by someone who needed the pain of it.

The letters rough, uneven, desperate:
*I LOVE YOU — I'LL FINISH IT*
*WE'LL MEET IN PARADISE*
And below, the signature that changes everything:
*WARBOY*

Catalina's hand flies to her mouth. Her knees buckle. She catches herself on the tree trunk — the same trunk two boys carved their initials into years ago — and a sound comes out of her that isn't a word. Her fingers press into the bark hard enough to leave marks of her own.

She knows that name. Everyone knows that name now. The fighter who moves through the underground pits like death itself. The boy with dead eyes and no mercy.

Her son's best friend.

Her son's love.

Gone.

"Oh, Jack," she whispers. "What have you become?"

The grave doesn't answer.

Baby Boy doesn't answer.

But somewhere in the Sulu Sea, the fight is beginning.

---

# The End

## "All children, except one, grow up."
### - J.M. Barrie, Peter Pan

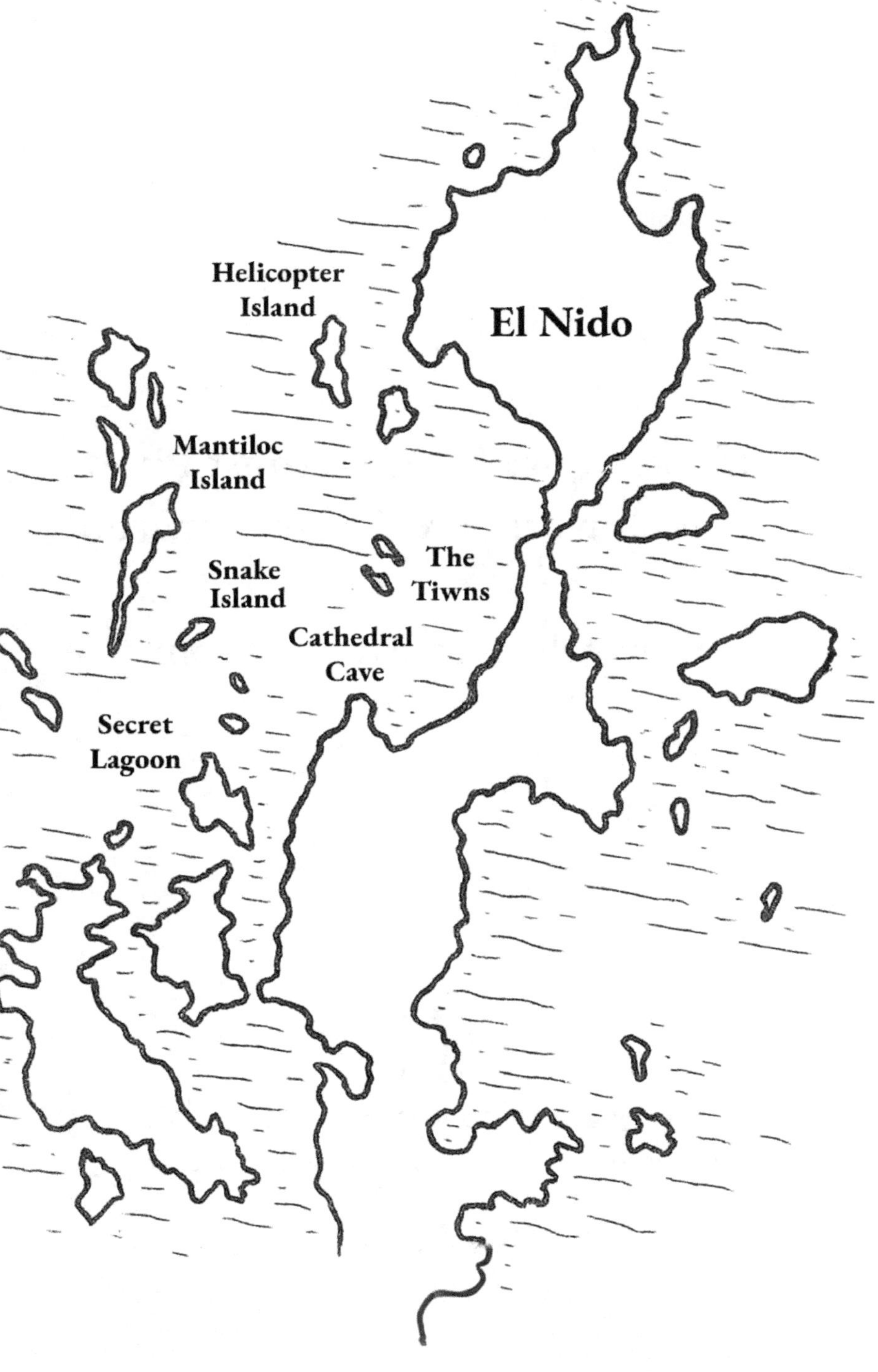

Helicopter
Island
El Nido
Mantiloc
Island
Snake
Island
The
Tiwns
Cathedral
Cave
Secret
Lagoon

# If you enjoyed The Stardust Pirates, Please leave us a review on Amazon!

www.thestardustpirates.com